Ben pulled a folded piece of paper out of his back pocket. Then, with a slow movement, he extended it toward Nikki. "It read 'Return the article and she will remain safe.'"

"She?" A wave of fear raised goose bumps along her arms. "Who is *she*?"

"There is only one *she* they could mean—you."

"We haven't seen each other in over two years, Ben. Until this afternoon, we've had no contact at all. And that was a coincidence. I don't know what this is about, but they must mean someone else."

He shook his head. "I don't think our running into each other was a coincidence at all. I think someone arranged it."

"What is this article they're talking about, anyway? What's going on, Ben? Why are you so worried?"

Nikki watched a struggle play across his face. Fi̶̶ he spoke in a low voice. "I don't want t̶̶ any more than you already a̶̶ don't know."

The memory of being wat̶c̶̶ wave on the beach. She gla̶̶ ̶̶̶osed patio curtains again. Was so̶̶ ̶̶ut there now? What had Ben done? Who had he run afoul of?

Books by Virginia Smith

VIRGINIA SMITH

A lifelong lover of books, Virginia Smith has always enjoyed immersing herself in fiction. In her mid-twenties she wrote her first story and discovered that writing well is harder than it looks; it took many years to produce a book worthy of publication. During the daylight hours she steadily climbed the corporate ladder and stole time to write late at night after the kids were in bed. With the publication of her first novel, she left her twenty-year corporate profession to devote her energy to her passion— writing stories that honor God and bring a smile to the faces of her readers. When she isn't writing, Ginny and her husband, Ted, enjoy exploring the extremes of nature— skiing in the mountains of Utah, motorcycle riding on the curvy roads of central Kentucky and scuba diving in the warm waters of the Caribbean. Visit her online at www.VirginiaSmith.org.

VIRGINIA SMITH

INTO
the DEEP

Steeple
Hill®

Published by Steeple Hill Books™

STEEPLE HILL BOOKS

Steeple
Hill®

Recycling programs
for this product may
not exist in your area.

ISBN-13: 978-0-373-44413-7

INTO THE DEEP

Where can I go from your Spirit? Where can I flee from your presence? If I go up to the heavens, you are there; if I make my bed in the depths, you are there.

—*Psalms* 139:7–8

For Ted, my dive buddy and best friend

Acknowledgments

I owe a debt of gratitude to many people for helping me with this book. Thanks to author Elizabeth Ludwig (www.elizabethludwig.com) who helped me with the Spanish phrases. *Gracias, amiga!* The members of the Utah Christian Writers Fellowship are a constant source of encouragement, and never fail to suggest ways to improve the story. You guys are great! My mom, Amy Barkman, proofread the manuscript on short notice. Thanks, Mom! My editor, Tina James, made so many insightful suggestions that resulted in a much stronger book than the one I wrote initially. Thank you for making me a better writer, Tina. My agent, Wendy Lawton, is not only a terrific businesswoman, she's the most encouraging agent in the industry. Thanks, Wendy. My husband not only helps me scout out new ideas for my books, he's a terrific dive buddy as well. Ted, I appreciate you more than I can say.

And of course, the biggest thanks goes to my "heavenly Dad," who has showed me the most incredible sights imaginable as I've donned scuba gear and traveled *Into the Deep.* How anyone can view His handiwork and still question His existence is beyond me.

PROLOGUE

October 13
Mexico

At the sight of the morning paper, a lump of ice dropped into Ben Dearinger's stomach. His brain did a quick translation of the Spanish headline screaming across the front page.

LOCAL MAN FOUND DEAD
DRUG CONNECTION SUSPECTED

Cesar Ramirez, the owner of Blue Waters Scuba Shop and Ben's boss, tapped the newspaper on the sales counter with a sturdy finger. "I worry about you last night, amigo." The trademark smile that normally split the man's darkly tanned face was absent, replaced by a concerned frown. "You hear nothing? No guns?"

"No, nothing." Ben swallowed against a dry throat. "Why? Did it happen nearby?"

"*Sí.* Two businesses were vandalized on this road last night." Cesar pointed southward down the beach. "And the man was killed not a kilometer from here. That way."

His finger switched to point up the beach in the opposite direction.

Ben's brain kicked into overdrive to translate as he scanned the article, searching for the victim's name. *Sergio Perez Rueda*. Though bright Mexican sunlight flooded through the dive shop windows, the room darkened as Ben's head started to spin. He took a backward step and slumped against the wall beside a rack of scuba tanks.

Cesar stepped toward Ben, hand outstretched. "What is it, amigo? He was a friend of yours, this Sergio?"

Ben scrubbed at his forehead, thoughts whirling. "No. I've seen him around, but I barely knew him. He…was here last night." Ben jerked his head toward the run-down two-room apartment he rented from Cesar at the back of the scuba shop. "For less than five minutes. He came to the door and asked to use the *baño*."

Ben had been sitting on the back porch, watching the sunset over the crystal blue waters when Sergio rounded the corner of the shop. He'd seen how jumpy the guy was, the way he kept glancing over his shoulder. His breath reeked of stale beer. Ben hadn't wanted to grant the request to use his bathroom, but what could he do? Be rude and tell the guy no? Instead, he'd led him into the tiny apartment and kept a vigilant watch outside the door until he emerged.

Ben lowered his voice, hating the question he was about to ask, but knowing he had to. "Should I contact the police, Cesar?"

His boss didn't answer at first. He ducked between the scuba regulator hoses dangling from overhead hooks like rows of rubber snakes. The whites of his eyes nearly disappeared as he narrowed his lids and considered Ben's question. Ben waited, breath halted in his chest, until finally Cesar shook his head.

"No, that is a bad idea. This Sergio, I heard about him. He is involved with bad people." His voice dropped to a low whisper. "Reynosa, I heard."

A chill zipped down Ben's spine. The Reynosa drug cartel had gained in strength and prevalence in the Mexican state of Quintana Roo in recent years. Their violent reputation had increased with reports of kidnappings and execution-style murders, both within their ranks and among those who opposed them. If the Reynosa cartel was responsible for Sergio's death, they might not look too kindly on a possible witness.

A car door slammed in front of the shop. Cesar's eyes darted in that direction. "Unless somebody asks, say nothing. That is my advice, amigo."

The first of the tourists scheduled for a morning of scuba diving entered the shop. Ben gave Cesar a single nod, then slipped into the back to begin readying the equipment they'd need to stow on the boat.

Though he had nothing but respect for the local police, whispered rumors of foreigners languishing in Mexican prisons had strengthened Ben's desire to stay below their radar during the three years he'd lived and worked as a dive master in Cozumel. And the Reynosa cartel… He suppressed a shudder. The more he thought about it, the more he became convinced that Cesar was right. Sergio had gotten himself mixed up with some nasty people, and now he was dead. Nothing Ben did or said could change that. But he was still very much alive, and he intended to stay that way.

Still, why had Sergio showed up at his place last night? Maybe it had nothing to do with the Reynosa cartel. Maybe he'd vandalized the two buildings Cesar mentioned and was running to escape the police.

On the other hand, surely the news report would have included the detail that a police chase had occurred. No, more likely he'd been running from someone else, someone not necessarily official.

Reynosa.

Ben shook his head. But then why stop to use his *baño?* It didn't make sense. Unless…

His pulse kicked up a notch as a possible reason occurred to him. With a quick backward glance toward Cesar, he slipped out the rear of the store and into his small apartment. A steady salt-scented ocean breeze filtered through the open window. Standing with his back against the door, he scanned the cramped room that served as bedroom, living room, dining room and with the aid of a microwave and coffee pot, the kitchen. Sergio had carried a canvas bag slung over his shoulder, which he'd taken into the second room of Ben's apartment, the bathroom. Was he being chased because of something inside the bag? Something he'd stolen? Money? Drugs? Acid surged into Ben's throat. Whatever it was, would Sergio have tried to stash it somewhere so he wouldn't be found with it?

Ben crossed to the *baño* and scanned the tiny room looking for anything that hadn't been here yesterday. Clean towels lay more or less folded on exposed shelves in one corner. No medicine chest, so his toothbrush and toiletries rested on the top shelf. The shower stall was a single unit—not possible to hide anything there. In fact, there was no place to conceal an item of any size.

I'm imagining things. He didn't stash anything here.

Ben turned to go. As he did, his gaze slid across the toilet.

It looked no different. But somehow, he knew. After all, there was no place else within the confines of this cramped room. Moving slowly, he lifted the tank lid. Peered inside.

On the surface of the water was a plastic bag.

He recognized the waterproof pouch instantly. He and Cesar used a similar one on the scuba boat to keep their valuables, such as cell phones and cash, dry. This pouch was folded slightly to wedge it inside the tank in a way that wouldn't interfere with the operation of the toilet. He couldn't immediately identify the item inside the clear vinyl bag. Not the cash or drugs he was expecting, though. Stomach in his throat, Ben lifted the bag out. He tore open the Velcro seal, unfolded the top flap and emptied the contents into his palm.

A flash drive.

He almost caved in to the impulse that urged, *Put it back. Pretend you never saw it.* But what if someone from the Reynosa cartel came looking for it? What would they do to him if they found it in his toilet?

Ben stared at it, his mind cataloguing a list of possible data that might be stored on this device. It would have to be something big, something worth a man's life. If it involved the Reynosa cartel, there was no telling.

The storage device gripped in his fist, Ben wrestled with his thoughts. One thing was certain. No way could he take this to the police. He'd be signing his own death warrant. And he couldn't leave it here, either. He had to ditch it, someplace it would never be found.

But where?

ONE

March 22
Key West, Florida

Double rows of razor-sharp teeth gleamed wickedly beneath a dead black eye. Nikki Hoffman could almost feel the chilly waters around her, the current pushing her toward powerful jaws....

"You wanna get up close and personal with a shark?"

Startled, Nikki tore her attention from the collage of photos tacked to a bulletin board and whirled around. A swimsuit-clad surfer dude, tanned and bare chested, had appeared from a back room of the small shop she'd just entered, apparently alerted to her presence by the jangle of bells on the front door. He flashed a blinding white grin that contained more teeth than the sharks in the underwater pictures she'd been studying.

"For a hundred bucks, I can teach you how to scuba dive and take you to a wreck where the sharks hang out." The grin became a leer. "Private lesson. You'd get my personal attention."

Nikki suppressed a shudder. Sharks gave her the

creeps. Especially the ones with two legs and an agenda that had nothing to do with salt water. She'd met plenty like this guy when she had lived in Cozumel.

With an effort, she pushed the thought from her mind. She'd made a promise to herself to look forward during this vacation, not backward. That was one promise she intended to keep.

"Thanks, but I gave up diving a couple of years ago." She unzipped the fanny pack that undoubtedly marked her as the tourist she was and fished through the contents. "I have a coupon here for a free sailing excursion."

"Free?" The guy's shoulders heaved with a laugh. "I don't think so. The bosses don't give anything away for free."

"This is Key West Water Adventures, isn't it?" Nikki glanced around the shop, looking for a sign. "This coupon is for a free excursion of my choice, up to a $100 value."

She pulled out the coupon and placed it on the counter. He examined it without picking it up.

Now that she looked at it again, this coupon didn't resemble the others in the welcome packet she'd received when she checked in to the time-share condo a few hours ago. It was just a black-and-white sheet of paper that might have been printed on a laser printer. But the logo at the top was identical to the one that adorned the sign hanging above the store's front door.

"Yeah, that's us, but I've never—" His gaze fixed on something over Nikki's shoulder and the confusion cleared from his face. "There's the boss now. You can ask him."

Nikki turned and looked through the window. The

shop lay midway down an L-shaped pier that stretched like a wooden finger into the bay. Beyond it, the mouth of the bay opened out into the blue Atlantic. Sunlight sparkled off the water's surface, momentarily blinding her. She blinked and caught sight of a boat moving slowly toward the end of the pier. A flag on top waved in the breeze, red with a white diagonal slash. The sight of the rippling silk sent a surprising wave of longing through her, so strong it halted her breath for a few heartbeats. A scuba flag.

Those days are long gone. And he's gone with them.

Swallowing back the surge of emotion, she snatched the coupon off the counter. "Thanks, I will."

Outside, the humid heat slapped at her with an open palm. The breeze carried a distinctive odor, a blend of salt and fish as familiar to Nikki as the smell of cookies baking in her mother's kitchen in Portland. She paused outside the shop and filled her lungs with the scent of the ocean. Many of the slips on the dock were empty, the boat owners probably enjoying this beautiful Friday afternoon. The wooden pier creaked as the remaining boats bobbed gently in the water, rocked by the gentle motion of this inlet. The scuba boat glided to a halt some distance away. She lowered the sunglasses from their resting place on top of her head and made her way toward the pier's end.

When the boat had been secured, two couples climbed onto the dock lugging scuba equipment and beach towels. They laughed and chattered as they shouldered bulky bags and headed in her direction. Music blasted from speakers on the boat. Jimmy Buffett, appropriately enough.

"Good dive?" she asked when they approached.

"Great dive," answered one guy with a wide grin. "We saw an eight-foot moray eel."

The girl walking beside him shoved his shoulder. "What a fish story. It was not eight feet long. But what about that school of yellow-striped fish? Does anybody know what kind they were?"

Then they were past, their voices carrying to Nikki as she neared the boat. The two men inside had their backs to her as they tidied up the deck. One picked up a weight belt and ducked into the cabin as the song ended. A few seconds later, Jimmy began singing about grapefruit and Juicy Fruit.

The second guy straightened and caught sight of her. "Hey, how's it going?"

"Fine." She spared him a smile. "Are you the owner?"

"I'm one of them." He shielded his eyes with a hand. "What can I do for you?"

Nikki extended the coupon toward him. "I dropped by to make a reservation for a sailing excursion with this coupon, but the guy in the shop didn't seem to know anything about it."

He glanced at it. "You're staying at the Pelican Resort, right?"

"That's right."

He unhooked a dive tank from its holder, nodding as he spoke. "Someone called and bought a gift certificate over the phone yesterday and had us deliver it to the Pelican. My partner took the call and told me about it. We don't sell many gift certificates."

Allison. A smile stole across Nikki's lips at the thought of her generous friend. As if letting Nikki use her family's time-share at no charge wasn't a generous enough birthday present.

The second man emerged from the cabin carrying a pair of fins. Nikki caught a glimpse of his profile as he crossed the deck in two long strides, then bent to store them beneath the bench.

"That must have been my friend," Nikki told the first man. "So, when can I—"

Shock snatched the rest of her question out of her mouth. For a second that lasted a lifetime, her world skidded to a halt.

She knew that profile.

Ben? Here?

Panic slammed her in the stomach, robbing her breath. A single, frenzied thought pulsed in her brain and catapulted her feet into action.

I can't let him see me.

She whirled and ran.

Even before his mind could fully register her presence, Ben jerked upright, his body reacting to the oh-so-familiar timbre of her voice.

Nikki.

It had been over two years, but he would recognize the woman running down the dock even if it had been forty. Her long legs, the familiar curve where her shoulders met her slender neck, even the way she ran with her hands pumping at her sides.

He dropped the fins, leaped from the boat to the dock and sprinted after her.

"Nikki, stop!"

She kept running. Ben kicked up his speed, ignoring the startled looks he collected from two men cleaning the morning's catch on the dock beside their boat. Pain raked his bare feet as they pounded the rough wood. She reached the edge of the pier and hesitated before turning toward town. Just a moment's hesitation, but it was enough. Ben overtook her before she'd gone five steps in that direction.

"Hold up a minute, will you?" He grabbed her arm and jerked them both to a stop, then stood panting and looking down into her face.

She'd changed. The smile lines at the corners of her mouth had deepened, and he saw the beginning of creases at the edges of the eyes she kept averted from him. She was a few pounds heavier, but the extra weight only softened the sharp angles he remembered. In Mexico, he'd fallen in love with a carefree girl, but the girl had grown up. Matured. She was a woman now.

A beautiful woman.

Her shoulders drooped with a nearly imperceptible sigh, and she raised her eyes to meet his. "Hello, Ben."

"Hello?" He vented a sudden surge of anger with a bitter laugh. "That's all you have to say after two-and-a-half years?"

A pause, and then her lips tightened. "I could say *let go of me,* instead." Her voice snapped with the spunk he remembered so well.

She jerked her arm away, and he realized he'd been gripping her so hard his fingers left red splotches. He started to apologize, but couldn't force the words out. If anybody owed anyone an apology here, it wasn't him. She'd packed up and left Cozumel while he was out on a dive. He had come home in the evening to find her clothes gone, the apartment somehow hollow and empty even though all the furniture remained. Her note gave no explanation, just two words—*Goodbye. Nikki.*

He tried to shove his hands in his pockets, realized he was wearing swim trunks, and folded them across his chest instead. "What are you doing in Key West, Nikki?"

Her eyes darted around as though searching for an appropriate answer. Then she lifted her shoulders in a slight shrug. "I'm on vacation. Just got in a couple of hours ago. I'm, uh, sorry for running like that. It was a shock. I wasn't expecting to see anyone I know." The brief smile she turned on him didn't reach her eyes. The polite smile of a stranger. She gestured toward his shirt, which bore the logo for Key West Water Adventures. "So, you live here now?"

The disappointment that surged through him at her impersonal conversation surprised him. So that's the way she was going to play out this awkward meeting. Polite. A chance encounter between two former friends.

Okay. Fine with him.

"Yeah, I moved here a few months ago."

"Still diving, I see." Was that a reference to their last argument, the one about settling down and becoming responsible? Though the afternoon air was warm, it seemed to Ben he was caught in a bubble of frigid air, one that surrounded him and this stranger he once knew so well.

He flipped his hands out, palms up. "Of course. You know me. I can't give it up."

She tilted her head and the sun glinted off her sunglasses. "I didn't think you'd ever leave Mexico."

A shudder threatened at the memory of his last fearful days in Cozumel. Ben pushed it away and awarded

Nikki a tight smile. He certainly wasn't going into his reasons for leaving. Not here. Not with her.

"The pay's better here," he said briefly, then changed the subject. "What about you? Where do you live now?"

"I moved back home to Oregon." Her gaze drifted sideways, as though planning her escape route. "I work for a finance company there."

"Sounds interesting." Actually, it sounded unutterably boring and *normal*. But that's what she said she wanted over two years ago during that last, heated argument. A normal life. He caught a flash of gold from a cross hanging around her neck. So, she hadn't gotten over her religious phase yet. He hesitated before asking the question that had plagued him periodically over the years. "Are you married? Have kids?"

She wrapped her arms around her middle, a clear signal that the question was unwelcome. The muscles in her slender throat moved as she swallowed. "I'm not married, no."

The wave of triumph that surged through him took him by surprise. She hadn't found everything she'd been looking for when she left, then. His heart suddenly and inexplicably lighter, Ben combed a hand through his hair. "Look, I've got to get back and help unload the boat. But how about if I take you to dinner?"

For a minute he thought she would agree. She hesitated, her lips parting. Then she closed them again and shook her head. "I, uh, have plans."

"Lunch, then. I'll get someone to cover the morning dive." He cocked his head and pasted on the smile that used to melt her resolve. "It'll give us a chance to catch up. I want to know what's happening in your life."

For a moment, something darkened her eyes, like a shadow of the feelings they'd once shared. But in the next instant, a door slammed shut in her face. The polite stranger's smile returned.

"Thanks, but I don't think that's a good idea." She took a backward step. "It was good to see you, though, Ben. Goodbye."

He was still trying to come up with some way to counter her obvious dismissal when she turned and walked away. Quickly, as though she couldn't wait to get away from him.

At least she'd said goodbye in person this time.

Nikki's back burned. She could feel his eyes on her as she hurried away. The clip-clop of her sandals changed tone as she stepped off the wooden dock and onto the street. She didn't dare glance backward, but her ears strained to hear footsteps coming after her. Would he follow?

Please, God, don't let him follow me.

Pain throbbed in her chest, a dull ache that she'd thought was long gone. Just like she thought her feelings for Ben had finally faded. Oh, she'd never forget him, that was a given. How could she, when his face loomed in her mind every day? But she'd really thought she'd gotten over her feelings for him. Or at least, wrapped them up and stored them in the deep recesses of her heart, where they couldn't hurt her anymore. One look at him, and she knew she'd been lying to herself.

Which made it even more important that she get away

from him. Her heart was no longer her own. It belonged to Joshua now.

And she would never tell Ben about the son he didn't know existed.

TWO

A shadow moved just beyond the circle of light that illuminated Nikki's patio. Her grip on her cell phone tightened. Was someone there? She sat straight up on the chaise longue, eyes searching the darkness, ears straining to hear anything out of place.

She heard nothing. Well, crickets and the distant sounds of splashing water and children's laughter coming from the direction of the resort's pool. But in the vicinity of her patio, everything was quiet. Peaceful. She forced her spine to relax.

"It's beautiful here, Mom." She settled back in her chair and continued her conversation. "Palm trees everywhere, and there's an orange tree in full bloom right outside my patio. You should smell it."

She inhaled the sweet, tropical scent deep into her lungs. Even though the sun had set half an hour ago, the air around her was still deliciously warm. After the harsh winter that had plagued Portland this year, Nikki relished the heat.

"I'm glad you're having a good time, honey." Her mother's voice was as warm as the air. "What did you do today?"

Nikki's brain conjured an image, but she pushed it

away. She'd struggled all afternoon to avoid thinking about Ben. Her first instinct after seeing him had been to run back here to the condo, repack her belongings and catch the first flight home. She still hadn't ruled out the possibility, but had finally decided to wait a day or so to make that decision. Tomorrow was her thirtieth birthday, so she might as well spend it as she'd planned, lounging in the sun, sipping chilled pineapple juice and losing herself in a good book. She'd be fine as long as she stayed far away from Key West Water Adventures, and Ben Dearinger.

She forced herself to speak normally into the phone. "I took a train tour of the island to get my bearings. Everything's really laid-back. Cats everywhere, and chickens roaming free on the streets. Joshua would love it." A pang of regret stabbed at her.

Mom's voice became stern. "Don't do that. You deserve some time alone. Joshua and I have a big week planned. He'll be fine."

I know. A tear pooled in the corner of her eye. *But I miss him.*

"What are you planning to do on your birthday?" Mom's cheery voice refused to let her become morose.

She steeled her voice against any quivering. "I'm not sure yet. I brought my passport, in case I can find a cheap day trip down to the Bahamas or something." She paused, missing her son more than she would have thought possible after only a few hours apart. "Let me talk to him one more time. I want to say good night."

"Just a minute. I'll get him."

"Thanks. And, Mom?"

"Yes?"

Nikki swallowed against emotions that threatened

to clog her throat. "I really appreciate you keeping him while I'm gone. Thank you."

The voice on the phone softened. "It's my pleasure to watch my grandson." A low chuckle. "Of course, I'm going to be worn out by the time you get back. It's been a long time since I've had charge of a two-year-old for a whole week."

A clatter sounded as her mother set the phone down. Nikki heard the music of Joshua's favorite DVD through the receiver, a cartoon about a race car. She didn't allow him to watch it before bedtime because it got him too worked up, but apparently the rules at Grandma's house were lax. Nikki closed her eyes, picturing him in his pj's, hair still damp from his bath, sprawled on the floor, his brown eyes fixed on the television set.

A soft sound interrupted her thoughts. An oddly familiar sound, but out of place. She jerked her eyes open. Her gaze zeroed in on a thick bush with lush, tropical blooms that bordered the private area surrounding her patio. Its branches rustled, though not even the hint of a breeze stirred the leaves on the orange tree in front of it. The hair along her arms prickled. Was someone there?

Nikki leaped out of the chair. Muscles tense, she strained to see beyond the patio light, into the shadowy darkness. Everything was still. With an effort, she forced herself to relax. She was imagining things. Or maybe it was a cat. There were plenty of those around. No need to be alarmed.

Still, she kept her eyes fixed on the bush as she stepped inside the condo and closed the glass door.

A beloved voice piped in her ear. "Mama, Speed Racer go *vvvrrrrooooooommmmm!*"

The strange movement forgotten, a swell of love brought a smile to her face. "He did? Tell me about it."

She settled herself on a plush couch cushion and focused on her son's enthusiastic retelling of the story they'd watched together a gazillion times.

But her gaze strayed repeatedly to the patio and the deep shadows beyond the orange tree.

Ben steered his bicycle through the front entrance of the Pelican Resort. He'd passed this place lots of times in the five months since he moved to Key West, but he'd never been inside. Lush foliage lined a narrow footpath beneath tall palms and mature trees with Spanish moss dripping from every branch. A half dozen two-story buildings lay scattered around the property in no discernable pattern. The randomness gave the place a casual, relaxed feel, perfect for island vacationers.

Ben hopped off the bike and walked it along the path, squinting in the dim light of decorative lanterns to read the letters mounted on the front of each building. According to the records at the dive shop, the gift certificate had been delivered to unit C-1. After a moment's search, he found building C tucked into a quiet corner at the back of the property. Eight condos in each building, four upstairs and four down. Number one would probably be on the ground floor. A light shone in the window of a corner unit and another in one of the units upstairs.

He left the bicycle on the pavement and stepped off the path beneath the thick, low-hanging branches of a tree. Long strands of lacy moss deepened his cover. He leaned against the trunk where he had a good vantage point of the corner of the building and the illuminated downstairs window.

With hands that trembled, he pulled the note out of his pocket and clutched it with a fist. Just the feel of the paper sent shivers sliding up his spine. It had been shoved under his apartment door for him to find when he got home from work. The words were proof that his first thoughts this afternoon had been right. Nikki showing up at the pier today had not been a coincidence.

Seeing her had given him the shock of his life. It was too much to believe that a woman from his past—his *Mexican* past—chose Key West for a vacation, and then within hours of arriving, just happened to show up at the shop where he worked. There were a dozen dive shops on the island. Why pick his? Nikki had seemed as surprised to see him as he was to see her. And she hadn't looked all that pleased, either. Was she in league with the Reynosa cartel? He would never believe that. Was she an unwitting pawn, then? The unsettling questions had plagued him all evening.

And then he found the note.

He raked a hand through his hair, the uncomfortable lump in the pit of his stomach becoming heavier by the minute. This was the most alarming in a recent series of disturbing incidents. A couple of months ago, he came home to find his apartment had been gone through. Nothing stolen, and nothing obviously out of place, so he'd had no reason to contact the police. But the moment he walked through the door, he'd spied evidence that someone had been there. A kitchen chair slightly skewed. The mattress on his bed almost imperceptibly cockeyed on the frame. The aspirin bottle on a different shelf of the medicine chest.

Then a week later, his car was broken into. He almost never drove the thing—nobody on the island did—so he didn't even realize it until one of his neighbors pointed out the busted window. That time he did call the cops, because he needed the police report for the insurance company. Nothing had come of it, though. Nothing had been taken from inside the car. The investigating officer told him it was probably teenagers, drunk or high and looking for something to hock.

After Cozumel, Ben wasn't so sure.

Now he had proof that his paranoia was founded on fact.

He snatched a handful of Spanish moss and crushed it with his fist. But what could he do about it? He didn't like living with this jumpy, paranoid feeling, searching every stranger's face, wondering if they were on Reynosa's payroll, but he couldn't risk going to the police. He'd end up as gator bait, face down in a swamp somewhere. No, it was better to mind his own business until they figured out he was no threat and left him alone.

He slid the folded paper between his fingers. That had been the plan for the past few months, anyway. The note changed everything. Upped the ante to a price he couldn't afford to pay.

A movement caught his eye, a dark place in the shadows at the side of Building C. He stiffened, his attention pricked to high alert. Was that shadowy form a person? He stared at the spot, straining his eyes to differentiate between shades of black and blacker in the foliage. Nothing moved.

His tense muscles started to relax, but in the next instant, he jerked upright. The bushes rustled, and this time he glimpsed the figure of a man. Just for a second, and then the person was gone, moving quickly away from Building C. He looked as though he'd just come from around the back of that first condo, the one with the light in the window. Thoughts whirled in Ben's brain. Why would someone sneak through the bushes instead of walking out in the open? Kids on vacation, maybe, playing hide-and-seek? No, the figure had been too tall to be a child. A maintenance man, maybe?

At nine o'clock at night? No way.

Ben's mouth went dry. Nikki was in that building, probably in that very condo on the end. Ben couldn't believe her presence in Key West was a coincidence any more than he believed the man slinking away from her building was just taking a nighttime stroll through the bushes. So either the man had been visiting Nikki openly, or he'd been there for a more sinister reason.

His feet sprang into motion before he fully decided to act. He ducked under the tree branches and sprinted toward Building C. In the breezeway, his brain barely had time to register the number 1 on the door before his fist assaulted the wood. He beat the door in tempo with his pounding heart.

If anything had happened to Nikki, he'd never forgive himself.

THREE

Nikki had just pressed the button to end her call when—

Boom! Boom! Boom!

Startled, her fist tightened around the silent phone as she shrank against the couch cushion. Her gaze flew toward the front door. The uneasy feeling from the patio returned, magnified a hundredfold and swelling even further with every insistent beat on the sturdy wood. Who in the world could it be? She didn't know a soul in Key West. No one except...

"Nikki, are you all right?"

That voice, so achingly familiar, echoed inside her like the pounding echoed through the entry hall. Ben. She hugged the phone to her chest.

Oh, Joshua, your daddy is here. I so badly want to tell him about you. But I can't. I won't.

She'd struggled with that decision two-and-a-half years ago, and she'd made the right choice. Ben made no secret of the fact that he never wanted to settle down, never wanted to have a family. If he'd discovered that she was pregnant, he would have "done the right thing." He would have insisted on marrying her and settling down to help her raise their child. She couldn't bear to force him to give up the lifestyle he loved and watch the resentment grow deeper in his eyes as each year passed.

"Nikki, it's Ben. Open the door."

Indecision kept her pinned to the sofa. She should have known he would follow her here. If only she hadn't run into him on the pier. No good could come of a reunion between them.

And yet, he was part of her past, an important part. Far more important than he would ever know. She couldn't deny that seeing him again had awakened memories—and feelings—she'd tried to bury years ago.

She stood and crossed the room to stand in front of the door.

"What do you want, Ben?" She pitched her voice loud to carry through the thick wood.

The incessant pounding ceased.

"Thank goodness." The relief in his voice was obvious. Though why he would sound so relieved to find her at home, she couldn't imagine. "Let me in, Nikki."

"I—" She placed a hand on the door and closed her eyes while conflicting impulses did battle inside her. Finally, she swallowed. "I don't think that's a good idea, Ben. It's late. Go home."

"It's not what you think." The door handle rattled. "You've got to let me in. Please."

Something in his voice weakened her resolve, something she didn't remember ever hearing in the months they spent together in Cozumel. Was it…fear?

After one more moment's hesitation, she twisted the dead bolt. The lock slid open with a loud click. The door swung inward silently.

Her heart launched into a traitorous thundering as she

took in the details she'd been afraid to notice this afternoon. The same Ben, yet different. Or was it just that she was accustomed to seeing those lips in miniature, on Joshua's face? The eyes that swept over her now were the identical green-brown color of her son's, only with a depth and intensity unknown to a two-year-old. The sturdy jaw. The tiny crease just below the place where his lower lip blended into his chin. Nikki clutched the door handle and hoped he didn't notice that her grip was the only thing that kept her from wavering on unsteady knees.

Ben's gaze swept the room behind her. "Are you okay?"

What an odd question. She glanced over her shoulder to follow his gaze but saw nothing out of place. "Of course I'm okay. Why wouldn't I be?"

He ignored her question. "May I come in?" He must have seen the hesitation on her face, because he added an insistent, "Please, Nikki. It's important."

Though alarm Klaxons sounded in her brain, Nikki took a backward step and allowed him to enter. When she closed the door behind him, he leaned past her to twist the dead bolt. She shot him a startled look.

"Humor me."

He offered no explanation. She followed him into the living room and watched as he stood in the center of the room to examine it from all angles. He crossed to the patio door and slid a metal locking rod into place at the top of the frame. Nikki hadn't noticed the locking device when she came inside before.

Ben pulled the drawstring to close the curtains, then turned and nodded toward the hallway. "Mind if I take a look in the bedrooms?"

Indignant, she opened her mouth to protest, but at the look on his face, closed it again. His lips formed a rigid line, with deep creases at the corners of his mouth. It *was* fear she'd heard in his voice at the door. She glanced toward the closed patio curtains, and the uneasy feeling she'd experienced earlier returned.

She gave permission with a jerk of her head, but remained in the living room. After he'd investigated both bedrooms, he returned. His expression was calmer, a touch more relaxed. The muscles in Nikki's stomach loosened a fraction.

"You want to tell me what this is all about?"

He crossed into the kitchen and checked the lock on the window before answering. "I wanted to make sure you were okay, that's all. You know, a single woman, traveling alone. You can't be too careful."

The explanation fell lamely into the empty space between them. Nikki folded her arms across her chest and gave him a stern look. The same look she gave Joshua when he was being naughty.

Ben's head fell forward. "Okay, that's a lie. I—" He swallowed and nodded toward the living area. "Maybe we'd better sit down."

The impulse to refuse died before she could put it into words. In all the months they spent living together in Cozumel, she couldn't remember ever seeing him wear such a serious expression. Without a word, she retreated across the room and seated herself in the over-stuffed chair on the far side of the sofa. Ben followed and dropped onto the cushion near her.

"I looked up where you were staying." He stared at his hands while he spoke. "When I was outside, trying to decide whether or not to knock on the door, I saw a shadow. Looked like someone sneaking around the corner of this building. I wanted to make sure you were okay."

So, someone *had* been there, watching her from the darkness beyond the orange tree. Nikki shuddered and rubbed her arms with her hands. "But why were you here at all?"

He hesitated, then straightened his long legs to pull a folded piece of paper out of the back pocket of his shorts. A struggle appeared on his face as he unfolded the paper. His eyes moved as he studied it. Then, with a slow movement, he extended it toward her.

She took the note. Wrinkles spidered across the paper, as though it had been crushed in a fist. The words, scrawled in blue ink, were in Spanish.

Regresa el artículo y lo seguirá siendo seguro.

Though she'd lived in Mexico with Ben for six months, she'd never become fluent in Spanish. And she hadn't spoken the language at all in the two-and-a-half years since she moved back home. She translated the words slowly.

"Return...the article...and..." She glanced up at him. "What does *lo seguirá siendo seguro* mean?"

Ben didn't meet her gaze. "It says, Return the article and she will stay safe."

"She?" A wave of fear raised goose bumps along her arms. "Who is *she?*"

"There is only one *she* they could mean." His hands clenched in a tight knot. "You."

Prickles of alarm inched up her spine. "That's ridiculous." He glanced up at the sharp tone in her voice. "We haven't seen each other in over two years, Ben." Nikki forced herself to speak calmly. "Until this afternoon, we've had no contact at all. And that was a coincidence. I don't know what this is about, but they must mean someone else. Your girlfriend, maybe."

"I haven't had a girlfriend since you left Cozumel."

A wave of pleasure warmed her insides at that news, but Nikki ignored it. "Then a friend, or someone you work with."

He shook his head. "I don't think our running into each other was a coincidence at all. I think someone arranged it. Are you sure you didn't know I was in Key West?"

"I thought you were still in Mexico." She held his gaze and spoke truthfully. "If I had known you were here, I wouldn't have come."

Guilt stabbed at her when he winced. She looked away. Brutally cruel words, perhaps, but she had no choice. Their relationship had been severed some time ago, and it must remain that way.

"What is this article they're talking about, anyway?"

"Nothing."

"Obviously it's not *nothing* if they want it back badly enough to threaten someone over it." She narrowed her eyes. "You didn't steal anything, did you?"

"Of course not." His hands sliced through the air in an impatient gesture. "That isn't important. What is important is that someone arranged for you to be here, in Key West, and we need to figure out who did it."

"I told you earlier. I'm here on vacation. A friend from work is letting me use her father's time-share."

He twisted his lips, clearly not buying the explanation. "Why didn't your friend come with you?"

"Because she hasn't been with the company long

enough to take a vacation, and her father couldn't find anyone to rent the place this year. She's letting me use it to celebrate my birthday. And that certificate was a birthday gift. It was a coincidence that the shop she called happened to be the one where you work."

"You came on a vacation for your birthday *alone?*" The words were heavy with skepticism. "The Nikki I used to know would have gotten a group of friends together to help her celebrate. She would have had people sleeping on the couch and in sleeping bags and even on lawn chairs."

I'm not the Nikki you used to know! She wanted to snap the words, but bit them off. The Nikki he knew had been twenty-seven, fun-loving, without a care in the world. Now she was a thirty-year-old single mother struggling to raise an active two-year-old alone, with no one—except her mother—to help ease the burden of responsibility. She'd lost touch with all her former friends, and she was too busy and too tired to make new ones. Joshua took all her spare time. And he was worth every minute.

Nikki rose from the chair and rubbed a chill out of her arms as she crossed to the kitchen. She opened cabinets until she found the one with glasses in it and took down two short ones. The pineapple juice she'd bought at the grocery store earlier was thoroughly chilled now. She wasn't really thirsty, but she needed to do something with her hands.

Ben followed her and perched on a tall chair at the high counter that separated the living area from the kitchen. "Listen, do me a favor, would you? Call your friend. Ask her why she chose Key West Water Adventures for the gift certificate."

Though she wanted to refuse outright, it was a reasonable request. The numbers on the stove clock showed 11:10 p.m. That meant it was only 9:10 p.m. in Portland. Allison would still be up. "Fine. I will."

She plopped a glass of juice on the counter in front of Ben before going for her cell phone. When she returned, he sat staring at the yellow liquid with a contemplative expression. Heat threatened to rise into her face. It was Ben who had gotten her hooked on pineapple juice in Cozumel. Joshua loved it.

With jerky gestures, she flipped open her phone and located Allison's number.

The call went to voice mail.

"She's not answering," Nikki told Ben as she hung up without leaving a message.

A frown creased Ben's brow. "Isn't that weird? Why wouldn't a friend take your call?"

"It's Friday night. She's probably out on a date or something." She set the phone on the counter and sipped from her juice glass. "I'll try her again later, but I'm telling you, it's a useless effort. You may not believe in coincidences, but I do."

He placed an arm on the counter and leaned toward her. "All I know is you showed up at my work after more than two years without a word, and the same day someone shoved a threatening letter under my door. Coincidence or not, I'm staying here tonight."

Now heat did flood her face. "That is so not happening."

When the realization of what he'd just suggested set in, matching red blotches appeared on his tanned cheeks. His gaze dropped, and it took Nikki a moment to realize he was staring at her necklace. She plucked at the chain and held the cross between her fingers.

He cleared his throat. "I didn't mean it like that. This condo has two bedrooms and a couch. I'll sleep on one of them."

A heavy silence fell between them. The thought of Ben sleeping in the same town would probably have kept her awake all night anyway. To have him in the same condo, on the other side of a door?

No.

Her fingers tightened on the cross. "What's going on, Ben? Why are you so worried?"

Nikki watched a struggle play across his face. Finally, he spoke in a low voice. "I don't want to involve you any more than you already are. It's safer if you don't know."

The memory of being watched crept over her like a wave washing up on the beach. She glanced toward the closed patio curtains again. Was someone out there now? What had Ben done? Who had he run afoul of?

With a jerk, Nikki straightened her spine. It didn't matter. Ben Dearinger was no longer a part of her life. Whatever trouble he'd gotten into, he could get himself out of. She wanted no part of it. She would leave Key West tomorrow, first thing in the morning, birthday or not. Forget the vacation. Forget the beach. She just wanted to go home, to safety and to Joshua.

She picked up his untouched glass and slung the juice in the sink. "You need to leave now."

"Nikki, I—"

His protest died in the face of the glare she turned on him. With a resigned sigh that sounded more like a huff, he reached near the telephone for the pen and notepad with the resort's logo. He jotted a number on the top sheet and shoved it across the counter in her direction.

"My cell phone. Call me if you hear anything weird. Even if it's just the wind blowing."

Though she would never admit it, having his number made her feel a tiny bit better. She followed him to the door. When he'd crossed the threshold, he turned. His mouth opened, then he hesitated as though he changed his mind about whatever he'd been about to say.

"Goodbye, Nikki. Lock the door behind me."

Any words she might have said were impossible. Her throat was too tight. She searched his face, memorizing the features she had never forgotten, and then gave a single nod before closing the door.

Not only did she lock the dead bolt, she shoved a chair from the dinette set beneath the handle. Then she rummaged in the kitchen drawers for the largest knife she could find. No doubt she wouldn't get a minute's sleep tonight. That was okay. She'd sleep on the plane tomorrow, on the way home to Oregon.

In the breezeway outside Nikki's door, Ben waited until he heard the lock click into place. A slivered moon cast white light across the resort grounds, but deep shadows darkened the areas beneath the many trees. He made his way to his bicycle, tense knots in his gut.

Nikki hated him. And he had no idea why.

No, *hate* was too strong a word. He hadn't sensed any strong emotion from her at all, other than an intense desire to get rid of him as soon as possible. Which wasn't fair. What did he ever do to her? Nothing, except be honest with her. Hadn't he told her right up front, before she moved into his Cozumel apartment, that he wasn't interested in a permanent relationship? That if she was looking for a husband, she should return to the States with her friends and leave him to his carefree life in Mexico?

He walked the bike over the winding path toward the resort entrance, his mind filled with memories of the pretty blonde tourist who came into the dive shop with her friends. They'd wanted to go snorkeling in Cozumel's crystal clear waters. The attraction had been instant and mutual. Ben and Nikki spent every minute together for the next week, and when her friends left to go home, she stayed. Quit her job over the phone, had her roommate send her belongings to her mother's house for storage and slipped easily into the life of a beach bum. His life.

Then she started going to that church and all the problems started.

Ben reached the main road. He waited for the traffic to pass, then swung his leg over the bar of his bicycle and planted a sandaled foot on the pedal. The bike picked up speed as he pedaled, generating a warm, salt-scented breeze to ruffle his hair.

Apparently she hadn't gotten over her religious phase in the years since she left. She'd clutched that cross like a talisman. Like he was a vampire and she needed protection against him. Which was ridiculous. They might not have parted on the best of terms, but surely she knew he would never hurt her.

But apparently, there was someone who would.

Sweat broke out on his forehead. The Reynosa drug cartel wouldn't hesitate to kill if it accomplished their purposes.

Even an innocent. Even Nikki.

And he would be responsible.

He reached a decision. With a quick glance over his shoulder to check for traffic, he executed a U-turn. Even if it meant spending the night beneath one of those moss-covered trees, somebody had to watch out for her, no matter what she said. Because she had no idea who she was dealing with.

But he did.

FOUR

Ben arrived at the dock for work early the next morning. He wedged the front tire of his bicycle through the steel rack at the end of the pier and threaded the bike chain around the frame. A wide yawn took possession of him for a moment, and he was too exhausted to fight it. He'd finally fallen asleep, against his will, sometime after four. An angry resort groundskeeper had mistaken him for a transient and kicked him awake at seven. Though he'd been chased off the resort property, a quick inspection of Nikki's building showed nothing out of place. At least, the door hadn't been broken down or anything.

He unstrapped his backpack from the bike and shouldered it as he stepped onto the wooden pier, heading for the dive shop. Actually, he felt a little stupid for spending the night there. His fears in the darkness last night seemed unreasonable today with bright sunlight sparkling on the constantly moving waters of the bay. Nikki was probably right. Her being here was a coincidence. More than a million tourists visited Key West each year. Plus, he worked for the biggest water sports shop on the island, and they maintained a top-notch

Web site. Anyone wanting to find out about booking an excursion long distance would naturally contact them.

But what about that note?

Ben's step faltered as he passed a twenty-two-foot sailboat getting ready to leave the pier. Okay, the note could be explained, too. Somehow the Reynosa people had found out about Nikki's visit. Or…maybe they'd witnessed the encounter on the pier. He'd long suspected they were keeping close tabs on him. Yeah, that was probably it. They jumped on the opportunity, decided to use her as another scare tactic to force him to act.

But there was no way they could know for sure he had the flash drive. They were guessing, hoping to force an admission out of him. The best thing he could do was treat this attempt like the others, and ignore it. As long as he didn't confirm their guesses, he and Nikki would both be safe.

His course of action decided, the confidence returned to Ben's step as he continued down the pier. Up ahead, he saw activity around the *Sally Jane,* the larger of the two dive boats owned by Key West Water Adventures. He bypassed the shop and went to the edge of the pier.

Tyler, co-owner of the shop and dive master on the *Sally Jane,* stood in the boat, snapping a diving cylinder into white plastic tank holders. On the dock, a cart with one more cylinder waited nearby. Ben dropped his backpack on the pier and grabbed it. When Tyler turned around, Ben handed the tank into the boat.

"Hey, man. You're here early." Ben nodded at the nineteen cylinders already secured. "I would have helped if you'd just waited a minute."

"No problem," Tyler assured him. "I wanted to get a jump on the day. Now that you're here, could you grab the weight belts? We've got eight divers this morning, all renting equipment."

"Sure thing."

Ben scooped up his backpack and tossed it onto the empty metal cart. He started toward the shop, pulling the cart behind him.

"Oh, yeah," Tyler said. "When I came in this morning there was an envelope on the floor. Had your name on it."

Ben stopped. Though the early morning sun was already working overtime to warm the air, a chill cooled his core. He turned. "My name?"

Tyler nodded, unconcerned. "Somebody must have shoved it under the door. It's on the counter."

Without another word, Ben hurried toward the shop. He left the cart in the center of the floor while he scooped up a manila envelope from the edge of the counter. Careful block letters spelled out his name in blue ink.

Fingers trembling, Ben bent open the metal clasp and unfolded the flap. A single piece of paper had been slipped inside. A sentence of Spanish scrawled expansively across one side.

Tráigalo al Mallory Square en la puesta del sol.

The second note in two days, but this one had the unmistakable sound of a demand. *Bring it to Mallory Square at sunset.* No doubt what *it* the note referred to.

Ben turned the paper over to look at the back side. When he did, his heart skidded to a stop.

The door behind him opened. He whirled, and then leaped forward to grip Tyler's shoulder. "Can you handle the morning dive without me?" He hadn't meant to shout, but his voice filled the small dive shop.

Tyler's eyebrows arched. "Sure, Ben. I'll give Jason a call. He can always step in on short notice." Concern colored his boss's features. "Is everything all right?"

"Yeah. No." Ben shook his head. "I don't know. I've got to go."

He scooped up his backpack and shoved the door open with his shoulder. He stuffed the paper in the pack as he sprinted down the pier toward his bicycle.

Nikki's resort was located near the center of the four-mile-long island. Ben arrived there in a matter of minutes. He didn't bother bringing the bike to a stop before jumping off in front of Building C. By the time the bike hit the side of the building and came to an abrupt halt in a flowering shrub, Ben was already beating a fist against Nikki's door.

"Nikki, it's Ben." When she didn't appear immediately, he pounded the wood harder. "Come on, Nikki. Open the door."

A sound came from inside. A scrape, and then the dead bolt turning. The door opened inward. Nikki stood inside wearing a pair of stretchy sweats and a rumpled T-shirt, a blue coffee mug in one hand.

Her lips twisted sideways. "This is becoming a habit, Ben."

Relief washed over him. She was okay. With an effort, he restrained himself from wrapping his arms around her in a protective hug. Instead, he took a step forward.

She didn't move. Her hair, inches from his nose, smelled of soap and flowers. A clean smell, outdoorsy and fresh.

"May I come in?" Her head started to shake, but he

spoke again quickly, before she could deny him. "Please, Nikki. I need to tell you something important."

Her sigh delivered a whiff of coffee-scented breath before she stepped back. "All right, but I don't have long."

He brushed past her and edged around a chair in the entry. *What in the world?* When she closed the door and turned around, she saw him looking at it.

"I, uh, propped it under the door handle last night." A flush colored her cheeks. "You had me pretty spooked."

"Good. You should be."

He entered the condo and plopped his backpack down on the breakfast counter. She went into the kitchen and stood on the other side, watching him with a cautious tilt to her head.

"I'd just about convinced myself that you were right, that you being here is nothing more than a coincidence." No need to mention his night spent outside her door. He slid the pack's zipper open and pulled out the paper. "Until I found this waiting for me at the dive shop this morning."

Nikki held his gaze as she took the paper. When she looked down, she gasped. Color drained from her face. "It's a picture of me. This…this was taken last night."

Ben looked at the black-and-white photo. It had been printed on regular paper by a computer printer. Even so, the quality was quite good, not grainy at all. In it, Nikki reclined on a lawn chair, a cell phone held to her ear. Her lips curved into an attractive half smile, and her eyes held a faraway look, her attention focused on whomever was on the other side of that phone. A stab of jealousy surprised Ben. Who commanded her attention so thoroughly?

He shook away the question. Behind her in the photograph, the patio door stood open. Through it, he glimpsed familiar-looking furniture. A quick look over his shoulder verified his guess. The picture was taken here, just outside on the patio.

"I thought so."

"I…I heard it. The camera." She closed her eyes briefly, then opened them and gave a shaky nod. "I remember hearing a noise that sounded familiar, but I couldn't place what it was. Now I know. It was the sound of a camera taking a picture."

"There's more."

He took the paper from her and turned it over to let her read the note on the back. Her eyelids narrowed as she translated, then looked up at him.

"What are they talking about, Ben? What do you have that these people want?"

"Nothing." His protest met a stony expression. He spread his hands. "Honest, I don't have it." He swallowed and lowered his eyes. "I did have it. Briefly. But they don't know that."

She crossed her arms. "Don't play games with me, Ben. Just tell me. What *is* it?"

For the span of a few seconds, they indulged in a stareathon that he had no chance of winning. Nikki wasn't about to back down until he came clean with her. Ben filled his lungs and blew the air out slowly. She had a right to know, especially since she'd been dragged into the situation against her will.

He slid the paper toward him and folded it over and over, mostly for something to occupy his hands while he told her about the night Sergio Perez Rueda was killed on a Cozumel beach not far from Ben's apartment. Then he described how he'd found the flash drive wedged in the tank of his toilet the next morning. Nikki's eyes widened appreciatively when he told her how he'd discovered that Sergio was a known associate of the Reynosa drug cartel. She had spent enough time in Mexico to know exactly how alarming that was.

"And what was on the flash drive?" she asked.

He pressed one last fold in the paper and avoided her eyes. "I didn't look."

A movement forced his gaze upward. She stood with her hands on her hips, shaking her head. "I know you better than that, Ben Dearinger. The curiosity would have driven you nuts. You looked."

He conceded with a dip of his head. She *did* know him well. "Okay, okay. I looked. But believe me, I wish I hadn't. The information on that drive was…" He selected a word carefully. "Incriminating."

"To you?"

"No. To someone important." He glanced over his shoulder, toward the empty living room area. A stupid gesture, but he couldn't help it. If anyone heard what he was about to say, it could be bad. Very bad. He lowered his voice. "Have you ever heard of Senator Adam Webb?"

Nikki reeled as though she'd been slapped. She couldn't have been any more stunned if Ben had told her that Santa Claus had just landed his sleigh on the roof. In fact, she'd believe that more easily than believing that Senator Adam Webb, the man who was daily on the front page of nearly every single newspaper in

the country, was somehow involved with the infamous
Reynosa drug cartel.

"I don't believe it."

"Yeah, well, it's true. There was a spreadsheet on the
flash drive, and it had two pages." Ben pulled out one of
the high-backed bar stools and slid into it. His forehead
wrinkled at a memory. "The first page didn't make sense.
Just row after row of numbers and dates, none of them
formatted. One column looked like it could have contained dollar amounts, but the others were too long, just
a string of unintelligible numbers. Then I saw the tabs
along the bottom of the screen. It said *Depósitos*."

"Deposits," Nikki said. She used spreadsheets at
work all the time. She could picture exactly what Ben
described.

He nodded. "The second sheet was labeled *Cuentas*. Accounts. At the top of that page were the names
and addresses of several offshore banks in the Cayman
Islands, each with an electronic routing number. Cayman
National Bank. Banco do Estado do Rio Grande do Sul.
First Caribbean International Bank. Then beneath each
bank were two columns. A name, and a number that
corresponded with one of those long numbers on the
first sheet." His fingers sketched invisible lines on the
countertop to demonstrate. "So the first sheet contained
deposits made to specific bank accounts, and the second
sheet identified the bank account's owner."

Nikki lowered her voice to match his volume. "And
Senator Webb's name was one of them?"

"Yeah. That's what got Sergio killed, Nikki. If anyone
finds out that Adam Webb is on Reynosa's payroll…"
He let out a low whistle.

He didn't have to finish his sentence. Nikki's imagination filled in the details. The famous senator had won his senate seat primarily because of his hard stand against the Mexican drug cartels and his efforts to stamp out their presence in his home state of Texas. He was widely acknowledged as one of the favorite candidates for his party's bid for the next presidential election. If it became known that Senator Webb was secretly being paid off by one of the most notorious cartels, it would be among the biggest scandals in the history of the country. Proof would certainly send the senator to prison, not to mention wreck his political future and those of many of his highly placed supporters, as well.

This was big. Way too big for them.

"You've got to call the FBI, Ben." She picked up the phone from the far edge of the counter and scooted it toward him.

Ben backed away like the telephone was poisonous. "I don't think so. I'd rather not get involved with the feds."

Nikki tightened her lips. That was so like Ben, Mr. I-don't-want-to-get-involved. He hadn't changed a bit. "You're already involved. With Reynosa. Personally, I'd prefer the FBI."

"I've got it under control," he insisted. "I just have to convince them that I don't have that flash drive."

She couldn't stop a sarcastic comeback. "Yeah, 'cause that's worked out so well for you up till now." She studied him more closely. "Why did they follow you to Key West, anyway? They must have some reason to suspect you've got that drive if they followed you all the way from Mexico."

He rubbed a hand across his chin. "I wish I knew.

I never let on at all. Just played dumb, even when they almost broke my jaw."

Nikki straightened. "They hit you?"

He winced. "That's an understatement. The day after Sergio died, my room was ransacked. Then that night I surprised a couple of men searching the scuba boat. They roughed me up pretty good." He ducked his head. "That's when I knew I had to leave Mexico. I hightailed it outta there the next day."

She pursed her lips and watched him. He must have mistaken her silence for an accusation, because he placed his hands flat on the counter and said defensively, "Hey, if I hadn't, I wouldn't be here. They'd have killed me for sure."

"Oh, I agree. I was just thinking that you leaving so suddenly probably looked suspicious. Either that or you didn't give a very convincing performance when they were, uh, *questioning* you."

His shoulders heaved with a soundless laugh. "Trust me. I did my best."

He sounded sincere. If this evidence was important enough to the Reynosa people to beat up Ben and then follow him to Florida, what did that mean for her? Her presence here was a coincidence, of that she was certain. How could it be anything else? But now she had alerted them to her existence. It seemed obvious that someone had seen them together on the pier yesterday and followed her back here, searching for a way to use her to pressure Ben to hand over that information. If they investigated her, it wouldn't take much to uncover her past relationship with Ben. And if they checked into her life any further, they'd find out that she didn't live alone. Her blood chilled at the thought.

Oh, why didn't I just stay home, where it's safe?

The idea to celebrate her birthday in the Florida Keys had been hers, though when she first mentioned it to her friend, she'd assumed that Allison would come with her. She'd thought they could split whatever cost was involved in using the place for the week and figured it would be affordable since it belonged to Allison's father. She'd never dreamed she would be given the use of the condo for free.

Even worse, she had almost brought Joshua with her. If she had…

Her coffee mug rested on the counter, the contents cold by now. She picked it up just to have something to hold on to. "Maybe you ought to just give them the flash drive."

He shook his head. "I can't do that. I really don't have it."

"What did you do, destroy it?"

He didn't answer and wouldn't look her in the face. Instead, he stared at the snapshot of Nikki from last night, his head bowed over the counter. She studied the top of his head. His hair needed to be trimmed, as always, but the curly, carefree style suited Ben in a way a more conservative cut wouldn't. She gripped the cool coffee mug to keep her fingers from smoothing down a dark, wavy lock. Joshua's hair had the same amount of curl.

Her throat tightened. If the Reynosa people had moved so quickly to take advantage of her presence in Key West, what would stop them from investigating her? A sick wave of panic threatened.

"Ben!" She spoke more sharply than she intended.

His head jerked upward. "What did you do with that drive?"

He leaned forward and held her gaze. "I left it in Mexico. And I don't want them to know I ever had it to begin with."

"Then what are you going to do about that?" She dipped her head toward the photo with the note.

Ben's lips became a tight line as he stared at the paper. She watched thoughts play across his face. Then he snatched up the note. "I'm going to meet them at Mallory Square at sunset. I'll talk to them, explain that I don't have whatever it is they're looking for. I'll convince them this time."

Nikki turned her back on him to dump the cold coffee into the sink. She should follow through with her plan. A phone call last night confirmed that there was a plane leaving the Key West airport at two-twenty this afternoon. The flight was full, but she had put her name on the standby list. If she didn't get on that one, she'd planned to rent a car and drive to the Miami airport. Anything to get off this island and away from Ben.

But now, she wasn't sure that was a good idea. What if she left and Ben failed to convince the Reynosa cartel that he didn't have the flash drive? They had followed him from Mexico to Key West. Would they follow her from Key West to Portland? If an ex-girlfriend looked like a good tool for blackmail, a child he didn't know about would be even better.

I can't lead them to Joshua.

She whirled around. "If that's the plan, then I'm going with you."

She had the satisfaction of seeing his jaw drop.

FIVE

Mallory Square was packed with people. Nikki hung close to Ben, wishing she could cling to his arm so they wouldn't get separated. On her train tour yesterday, she had visited the famous pier and snapped a few pictures of the chickens running free in the wide-open area where the nightly sunset celebration occurred. The place had looked big and empty during the day, but now an astounding number of people crowded into the square. A variety of music clashed in a cacophony of sound, both from street musicians and from a nearby bar. Performers of all kinds vied for attention, everything from performing dogs to tightrope walkers to a Houdini wannabe pulling brightly colored scarves seemingly out of thin air. Along the perimeter, rainbow-hued umbrellas arched over handcarts displaying an array of wares for sale.

"Is it always this crowded?" she shouted toward Ben.

He placed his mouth so close to her ear that she felt his warm breath on her cheek. "Almost always. But Saturday nights are busier than most."

A man jostled against her so hard he almost knocked her over. "Shorryboutthat." His words slurred together, and Nikki winced at his alcoholic breath. He was sucked into the mass of people before she could reply.

Ben reached down and grabbed her hand. "We don't want to get separated."

Wordlessly, Nikki nodded and tried to ignore the warmth of his touch, the familiar way her hand fit inside his. For a moment, a gap appeared in the crowd and she glimpsed the shimmer of water at the far end of the concrete pier. The sun hung low in the western sky, painting the clouds with Technicolor rays. Memories rushed over her, and she tried to ignore them. How many sunsets had she and Ben watched together in Mexico? If she allowed herself to reminisce, she could almost feel the sand beneath her bare feet and hear the call of the seagulls as they soared over the waves searching for their last meal of the day.

A brightly clad woman on a three-wheeled bicycle approached the edge of the crowd, a hand-lettered sign on the full basket proclaiming her to be the "Cookie Lady." The throng opened and accepted her into its embrace, and within seconds she was hidden from sight.

"How will we ever find the person who wrote the note?" Nikki asked. "We don't even know what he looks like."

Ben's eyes moved as he scanned the people who filed past the buildings that lined the square. "Don't worry. He'll find us."

His tone raised the hair on her arms. She tightened her grip on his hand and searched the faces of the people coming into the square. Most were smiling and didn't look at all threatening. Just tourists coming to enjoy Key West's famous sunset celebration, hoping to catch a glimpse of the elusive green flash that sometimes happened when the sun set into the ocean. Of course, she had no idea who she was looking for. There were tons of Latino people all around her, and besides, the person they sought might not be from Mexico at all. The Reynosa cartel probably had non-Mexican operatives in the United States.

Well, for certain they did. Senator Adam Webb was one of them.

The crowd continued to swell with more people than Nikki would have thought the square could hold, until the pier was packed full. People surged around them, and she found herself jostled sideways. She bumped into Ben and then was pressed full-length against his side. The contact sent a thrill through her and, from the intensity in the eyes that suddenly locked on to hers, through him, as well. Blood rushed to heat her face.

"Sorry," she mumbled, and dropped his hand in her hurry to peel herself away from his body.

Another shove pushed her away from him. In seconds, the crowd had closed the gap. Her pulse picked up speed as she lost sight of his dark, unruly curls. A wave of bodies pressed her backward, like a paper cup carried to the beach by the surf. She opened her mouth to call Ben's name—

A hand clamped over her mouth. Another grabbed her upper arm in a viselike grip. Before she could twist away, she was spun around and propelled deeper into the crowd.

Ben's attention was fixed on the crowd when Nikki released his hand. His first instinct was to sweep her close to him with a protective arm, but their history together stopped him. That and the fact that she obviously found his touch repulsive. He hesitated for just a second, but it was enough. Someone stepped between them, and then another person. Within seconds he could no longer see her.

A frantic fist squeezed his throat. He forced himself to relax. Common sense told him there was nothing to worry about, that it was easy to become separated in a crowd like this. Why didn't he think to fix a place to meet if they lost each other? He scanned the people in his vicinity, looking for her familiar blond head.

There! He was sure that was Nikki, but why was she moving away from him, farther into the mass of people swarming around the square?

Her head turned, and he caught a glimpse of her profile. He raised a hand and started to call her name, but then stopped. A dark head leaned close to say something to her, the man's short-cropped black hair a stark contrast to her shining locks. Fear tightened her features, and then she was gone, pulled farther into the crowd.

A heavy knot twisted his stomach. The Reynosa cartel had Nikki.

For an instant, he was frozen. Then he jerked upright. He couldn't lose sight of her. He pushed forward, shoving a man out of his way.

"Hey, watch it, buddy!"

Ben muttered an apology, but he was gone before the guy could have heard it, shouldering his way through the crowd, his gaze scanning the people in front of him. He caught the occasional glimpse of Nikki's blond hair through a gap in the multitude, and kept forcing his way toward the pier's edge.

When he arrived on the other end, the crowd thinned out slightly. A few people lined the waist-high railing at the edge of the pier, watching the sun sink toward the horizon. Most, though, were focused on the performers, oblivious to nature's show going on behind their backs. Ben skirted around a wooden cart strung with beaded necklaces, his gaze darting everywhere.

Then he spotted her.

Nikki stood a little apart from the crowd, a Latino man close beside her. Her body was pressed against the protective barrier that lined the edge of the pier. As Ben made his way in that direction, he saw that the man had a tight grip on her arm with one hand. The second hand was around her waist. Did it hold a weapon? He couldn't tell.

She caught sight of him as he approached. Their eyes locked. The fear Ben saw in hers left him cold. He tried to put as much assurance as he could into his smile. If he could just get his hands on that thug—

A voice at his side halted his step. "*Alto.*" *Stop.*

Ben stopped just in front of Nikki.

"We have some business, amigo." A high tenor, heavily accented, the tone light, almost pleasant. "You have something of ours."

Ben turned. The Latino man standing beside him was several inches shorter than him, with a muscular build and sun-darkened skin. Ben searched his features and sifted through his memory. He'd never seen this man before.

"I don't know what you're talking about." He tried to match the man's tone, but fear had tightened his throat. His voice sounded as though it was squeezed through a funnel. "Let her go."

The man acted as if Ben had not spoken. His head

dipped in Nikki's direction. "And now, we have something of yours. A trade is in order, yes?"

Ben's hands tightened into fists. "I told your buddies in Cozumel that I don't have whatever it is you're looking for."

"That is what I heard. But they did not believe you, and neither do I."

A couple walked between them and Nikki, and Ben twisted sideways to keep an eye on her. The man who held her saw his move and pulled her even closer. A visible shudder rippled through her body.

"Listen," Ben said, "you people searched my room in Mexico and my apartment here. If I had something of yours, you would have found it by now."

"Not if it was well hidden."

"Come on, that's ridiculous." Ben tore his eyes away from Nikki and faced the Reynosa operative. "Look, if I had it, I'd turn it over. I promise. Tell that to whomever you work for."

He didn't want to say the name *Reynosa* out loud. Not here. Not anywhere. If, by some miracle, they didn't know he'd identified them, he wanted to keep it that way.

"A friend of yours told us a story, amigo. He said he left something with you, something very valuable."

Ben's blood chilled. He hadn't told a soul about the flash drive. Nobody knew. Nobody except Nikki and…
"What friend?"

The man stepped closer. "Señor Rueda."

His mouth dried in an instant. So, Sergio had talked before he died. What had they done to him to pry that information out of him? Ben suppressed a shudder, his imagination running wild. "Sergio wasn't my friend, and he didn't give me anything." He tried to make his voice sound convincing, but even he could hear a note of uncertainty.

"No, but he left it in your room at the dive shop. We tried to keep you out of the conflict, amigo. We waited until you left your room the next day. But when we went to retrieve the item…" He held his hands out, fingers splayed. "It is our property. We want it back."

"Your friends in Cozumel didn't mention any of this." The shadow of an ache throbbed in Ben's jaw at the memory of his previous encounter with the Reynosa cartel when he'd caught them searching the scuba boat. "Why have your people waited so long to contact me? Why mess around with searching my place, busting out my car window?"

The man shrugged. "Mexican wheels turn slowly. You lived there. You know this." A smile crept onto his face as he glanced toward Nikki. He raised his voice loud enough for her to hear. "But I am not one to let an opportunity pass. The pretty *señorita* is an opportunity. So, if you will just turn over the item, my friend will release the girl. She can go home to her family. That will make her happy, yes?"

At his words, Nikki's eyes widened. She drew a sharp inward breath. Her gaze snapped to his face. What he saw there looked dangerously close to panic.

The smile on the man beside him deepened. "The *señorita* is very pretty, amigo. A shame to let anything happen to her."

The fingers gripping Nikki's arm bit into her flesh. From where he stood, Ben could see the reddened skin in the fleshy part of her upper arm. Then he noticed something else—the fingers of the thug's other hand were curved around her waist. He clearly saw all four of them. Impossible to hold a weapon and still grip her waist like that. The only thing holding Nikki captive was that thug's bare hands. If Ben rushed the guy, maybe he could break his hold.

Still, the tough guy had managed to manhandle her through the crowd once. He could certainly do it again. If Señor Mouth here, the one doing all the talking, delayed Ben for even an instant, she would disappear into the masses in a heartbeat. And if they took her away, would he ever be able to find her?

Ben made a decision. His attempts to avoid becoming entangled with the Reynosa cartel had failed. Now he'd endangered Nikki, too. And for what? Let them have their proof against the dirty senator. He wasn't going to do anything with the flash drive, anyway. He spoke loud enough for Nikki and her captor to hear.

"Okay, I'll give it to you."

Nikki's shoulders deflated as the breath whooshed out of her lungs. Señor Mouth nodded.

"A wise decision. Hand it over, and you will not see us again."

"I can't." Ben gulped as the man's face hardened. "I mean, not right this second. It's not here. I hid it in Mexico."

Señor Mouth cocked his head sideways and studied him through narrowed eyes. "Tell me where. I will make a phone call, and then we will wait. When the item is recovered, you and the *señorita* will be free to go." He reached into his pocket and pulled out a cell phone.

Ben shook his head. "You'll never find it on your own. In fact, it might not even be there anymore. It might have washed away."

"You hid it underwater?"

Either he was really quick, or the Reynosa people had already considered the possibility. Probably the latter. This guy looked like he'd been selected for brawn more than brains. Ben nodded.

He slid the phone back in his pocket. "Then you had better pray the tide has not swept it away. You will get it yourself." An unpleasant grin appeared on his face. "And we will keep your friend safe until you return."

Nikki watched him, her blue eyes intense as the ocean in a storm. He could catch an early morning flight to Mexico, hitch a boat ride to the dive site, retrieve the flash drive and turn it over to someone in the Reynosa organization by tomorrow afternoon. But there was no way he was leaving Nikki with this pair.

He scanned the constantly moving crowd around him. Through the entire conversation, nobody had paid any attention to them. The sun hovered inches above the horizon, and those in their vicinity were focused on watching. Tourists snapped pictures. A clown on stilts took small steps through the crowd, making his way to a less populated area of the pier.

"That's not how it's going to work," he told the Latino man.

Señor Mouth shook his head, laughing. "Amigo, you are not in a position to—"

He didn't have an opportunity to finish his sentence. At that moment, the clown drew alongside them. The people backed up to give him room to pass, and, as Ben expected, pressed close to the Reynosa operative. For no more than a second, the man's attention was diverted as he glanced over his shoulder to see who had pushed him. Ben cocked his arm forward and then landed an elbow right in the Latino's solar plexus. The man doubled over, gasping.

Ben wasted no time in dashing forward, intending to throw his arm around the neck of the one who held Nikki and pry him off her. But she was as quick thinking as ever and apparently anticipated his action. She raised her leg and stomped on the thug's foot. Though her effort would have had more effect if she'd been wearing those spiky heels she used to like instead of sandals, it served to startle her captor enough that his grip loosened slightly. At the same moment, she twisted sideways. He still held her arm, but now her body was not between him and Ben.

Ben lowered his head and charged with as much force as he could gather in the short distance. The top of his head connected with the guy's chin. That freed Nikki from his grasp. When she jerked away, Ben did the first thing he could think of. He shoved the startled man as hard as he could. His body tumbled backward, over the top of the waist-high railing, and landed with a sickening thud on the concrete. With an audible groan, the thug doubled up on the ground and rolled sideways. Fortunately for Ben, he rolled away from the railing. In the next instant, he disappeared over the edge of the pier.

The splash as he hit the water twelve feet below seemed to electrify the crowd. A woman screamed, and then another, and within seconds, people were shouting and climbing over the railing, trying to get to the edge of the pier to help the man up. Ben lost sight of Señor Mouth as the crowd surged forward.

He grabbed Nikki's hand. "Come on."

They pushed through the mass of people, holding

tightly to each other's hands. Ben knew he had no choice. There was only one way to end this nightmare. He had to return to Mexico and retrieve that flash drive.

SIX

Nikki clutched the armrest of Ben's old Ford and tried not to turn around again to stare at the headlights through the back window. Were they being followed? It was too dark to see the occupants of the car behind them. In the driver's seat beside her, Ben's glance kept going to the rearview mirror.

"Do you think they're back there?" Her question quivered.

He flashed a sideways glance toward her. "I don't think so. Most of the cars that followed us out of Key West have passed us by now."

They zoomed along U.S. 1, the wind from the open windows louder than the music that crackled through the speakers. On Nikki's right, an ocean of endless darkness stretched as far as she could see. They'd driven through Florida's Lower Keys and were nearing the end of the Seven Mile Bridge.

This is so not how I expected to spend my thirtieth birthday. Not who I expected to spend it with, either.

She stole a glance at Ben. He had acted bravely, even heroically, back on the pier. And not just when he attacked the man holding her. Her upper arm ached even now from the terrifying grip that had held her captive, and her heartbeat quickened at the memory of the rough fingers at her waist. In those moments when she'd lost sight of Ben, terror had nearly paralyzed her lungs, and she'd thought she might faint from fear. But the look in Ben's eyes when he found them, the assurance he'd communicated silently to her, had slowed her pounding heart. His presence gave her a sense of safety at odds with her surroundings.

Just like always.

Nikki pushed away the disturbing realization and focused her attention on the road before them.

After they'd forced their way through the crowd at Mallory Square, they'd run the few blocks to Ben's home. She barely had time to glance around the sparse, three-room apartment while he shoved a few things in a backpack and grabbed his car keys. Her request to go by the condo to pack an overnight bag was overruled. Though his terse tone irritated her, Nikki knew he was right. Everything vital—her credit cards, vacation cash and passport—was in the fanny pack she was wearing at Mallory Square, because she'd been too anxious to leave any identifying documents back at the condo. Even her suitcases had been stripped of the name tags. She whispered a prayer of thanks for that attack of paranoia. After the disaster at the pier, it was almost a certainty the Reynosa people would go to the resort. If they broke in and searched the place, all they'd find were her clothes and shoes, nothing with her address back in Portland.

But what if they know my name? The tendril of fear that had wound itself around her insides tightened. *If they know who I am, it wouldn't be hard to find out where I live.*

The bits and pieces she'd been able to hear of the

conversation between Ben and the man at Mallory Square came back to her now with frightening clarity. Not once had the Mexican man referred to her by name. Chances were they didn't know anything about her beyond the fact that she and Ben had known each other in Mexico and had met up again by chance yesterday afternoon near the dive shop where he worked.

But the more she thought about that, the less likely it seemed the meeting was coincidental.

What if Allison didn't send that gift certificate? What if they arranged it?

As though he could read her mind, Ben's voice broke into the silence. "Why don't you try your friend again?"

The cell phone was warm from being clutched in her hand. She rolled up her window so she could hear, and Ben did the same. When she pressed Redial and held it to her ear, she halfway expected to hear Allison's voice mail again.

"Hey, girl!" A familiar voice chirped in her ear. "I hope you're calling me from a seaside restaurant, where you're sitting across the table from a gorgeous hunk you picked up on the beach today."

The seat belt strap pressed against her shoulder as Nikki straightened. "Allison! Thank goodness you're there. I've been trying to call you all day."

"Yeah, I just got home a few minutes ago and saw I missed a few calls from you. Sorry about that. I forgot my phone again. I've been out shopping all day. You should see the *adorable* shoes I bought. Perfect for that red strapless number I got last month. You remember the one?"

"I remember." Nikki tried to filter the tension out of

her voice. No sense setting off an alarm back in Portland if she didn't have to. "Listen, Allison, I have a question. Did you send me a gift certificate for a water excursion for my birthday?"

A delighted laugh sounded through the phone. "That wasn't me. It was your mom! She wanted to give you a special birthday surprise. How cool is that?"

Nikki wilted against the seat back. Beside her, Ben glanced her way. Nikki smiled and mouthed, *My mom.* He blew out a relieved breath.

"I never thought of asking her," she told Allison. "What a relief."

"A relief? Why would you say that?"

Nikki closed her eyes to shut out the sight of Ben. "I can't explain right now. It's a little complicated."

A note of alarm crept into Allison's voice. "Complicated? Nikki, what's wrong? You sound funny. Is everything okay?"

Now was not the time to go into an explanation. Not with Ben inches away from her, listening to every word. But she needed to ask a favor of Allison, and she wanted to make sure her friend understood how important it was. And she couldn't mention Joshua by name.

The carefully planned lie fell easily from her lips. "Everything's fine, but I had an incident today that spooked me a bit. Somebody tried to mug me this evening. It's too complicated to go into right now, but I think the guy picked me out when I went to collect on that gift certificate."

"Nikki! That's terrible! Are you okay? Did they steal anything? If you need me to wire you some money, that's not a problem."

Warmth flooded through her at her friend's offer. "I'm

fine. They didn't get anything. I'm just a little shook up, you know?"

"I can understand that. I'd be freaking out."

"Listen, Allison, don't mention anything to Mom. I don't want to worry her. But could you do me a favor? Keep an eye on her. Give her a call tonight. Maybe drop by tomorrow and check on…things."

Beside her, Ben turned his head to give her a curious look. Nikki ignored him. The urge to call Mom was so strong it sat like a hot lump in her stomach, but she didn't dare. Joshua would want to talk to his mommy, and there was no way she could hide the fact that she was talking to a child with Ben listening to every word.

Allison's voice took on an edge. "Why would you getting mugged in Key West make you worry about your mother in Portland? What's going on, Nikki?"

She forced a laugh. "Oh, I'm just paranoid, that's all. But could you do it? Just make sure everything's okay. Please?"

"Of course I'll be happy to check on her and Joshua."

Nikki pressed the phone closer to her ear. Could Ben hear Allison's voice over the roar of the engine and the noise of the wheels on the road? His expression hadn't changed, so she didn't think so.

"Thanks, Allison. I really appreciate it."

"Now you're spooking me. Listen, be careful, okay? I mean, Key West is supposed to be pretty safe, but a woman traveling alone is a target for unscrupulous people. Don't go out by yourself at night."

Nikki poured more confidence than she felt into her voice. "Don't worry about me. I'm fine. I'll call you tomorrow."

When she pressed the button to disconnect the call, she stared at the blank screen.

Ben's question broke the silence in the car. "Your mother sent the gift certificate?"

She nodded. "As a birthday surprise."

"Well, that's one mystery explained, then. It really was just a coincidence that the Reynosa people saw us together yesterday and decided to use you as leverage." A muscle in his jaw bunched into a knot. "It worked, too."

"I guess it did."

He awarded her a tight smile. "Well, we'll be in Miami in a few hours. I'll take you to the airport, and you can get on the next plane home."

"What about you? Are you going through with it?"

Ben's teeth appeared and clamped down on his lower lip for a moment. Finally, he shrugged. "I'm going to Mexico for sure. After that, who knows? I wasn't kidding when I told that guy the flash drive might not even be there anymore. I hid it pretty well, but you know how strong the current is there." He flashed a quick smile her way. "You don't have to worry about it. You just go on home. I'll take care of everything."

Nikki stared straight ahead. Clouds blocked the moon and shrouded the landscape in darkness. The beams from their headlights illuminated the road between their car and the red taillights in front of them. Could she trust Ben to take care of things? No, she couldn't. Not that he wouldn't follow through with his plan, but Joshua was her responsibility, hers alone. As much as she wanted to hop on a plane tonight and head home to stand guard over him, she couldn't do that. Until that flash drive was in the hands of the Reynosa cartel, she had to assume they were looking for her. What if they were being fol-lowed right now? She cast a nervous glance over her shoulder at the line of headlights behind them. The last thing she could do was go home, where she would lead them directly to Joshua.

Actually, the right thing to do would be to retrieve the flash drive and turn it over to the FBI. Expose the crooked senator.

"You know, Ben, you really should turn the drive over to the FBI. The country needs to know about Senator Webb."

He shrugged, but didn't respond. Nikki studied his profile for a moment. Could she convince him? Maybe, but first she'd need to talk to the federal agents privately. They'd have to promise to protect her and Joshua and Mom. Give them a guard or put them in protective cus-tody or something.

Lord, what should I do?

The answer to her question became clear almost immediately. Until Ben had retrieved the flash drive, she could do nothing. With that drive in their hands, they had bargaining power.

She fixed her eyes on the yellow line in the center of the road. "I'm not going back to Portland. I'm going to Mexico with you."

The car jerked violently as the right-hand tires swerved dangerously close to the concrete barrier pro-tecting them from the dark, churning waters.

Ben steadied the steering wheel before he turned an outraged look on Nikki.

"What are you, crazy? You heard that guy back there. They were going to hold you captive until I got the flash drive to them. Do you really want to spend time getting up-close-and-personal with a couple of Mexican drug dealers? Because the next time they grab you, I don't think they're going to be so easy to get away from."

"That's exactly my point. If they're back there—" she inclined her head to indicate the line of cars behind them "—watching to see our next move, I don't want to lead them straight to Portland. I want to make sure this situation is resolved, or I'll be looking over my shoulder forever."

Ben had to admit there was some truth in her logic. "Okay, so you'll barricade yourself in a hotel in Miami until this thing is over. I'll call you when it's done, and you can go home then."

"Right, 'cause they don't have connections in Miami or anything." Her mouth twisted in a tell-me-another-one grimace.

"They probably do." He conceded the point with a nod. "But Mexico is *their* turf. We'll be a lot easier to spot there. And you can bet they'll be watching every flight into Cozumel."

She turned sideways in her seat to face him. "Come on, Ben. I know you better than that. You're not planning to fly to Cozumel. You wouldn't want to be that visible."

He wanted to deny her statement. She did *not* know him, not anymore. Not since she walked out on him without a word almost three years ago.

But in this case, she was right. Flying straight back to Cozumel would be stupid, and wasn't part of the tentative plan that had begun to form in his mind.

Nikki went on. "And since the next closest airport is Cancun, I don't think you're planning to fly there, either. They'd expect that. Mexico City would be the best place to make sure we're anonymous, because it's so big. But that's way too far to drive. So I'm thinking…" She folded one arm across her middle, propped her elbow on it and tapped her lips with a finger while she stared at him through narrowed eyes as though trying to read his thoughts. "Mérida," she finally said. "Smaller, but far less likely to be watched. We can pretend we're tourists, rent a car and be in Playa del Carmen in a few hours. Then we can hop on the ferry with the rest of the tourists for the ride over to Cozumel."

Ben stared through the windshield. *She does know me too well.* He didn't know whether to be amused or irritated.

He lifted his foot from the gas pedal to slow the car as they approached Marathon, the town that marked the halfway point through the Florida Keys. They were a little over two hours from Miami. He had that long to convince her to change her mind.

But even as the thought occurred to him, he knew it would be a wasted effort. Nikki had always possessed a stubborn streak wider than the Grand Canyon. Actually, that was one of the things he had admired about her when they first met. When she set her mind on doing something, she refused to be sidetracked.

Not that he'd always agreed with her. That whole church thing, for instance. Right at the end of their relationship, she'd insisted on hanging around that church in Cozumel, no matter how hard he tried to make her see reason. The more he thought about it in the months after she left, the more he became convinced those religious people were the reason she'd left Cozumel. Left him.

Ben clenched his teeth. His dad had been right about

church. Ben remembered the time when he was ten, when Dad blew into town on his Harley for one of his unannounced, infrequent visits. It was Sunday morning, almost time to leave for church, and Ben and Mom were just finishing breakfast. Dad had wolfed down the eggs and toast Mom fixed for him, using his fork between bites to emphasize his point.

"What do you want to drag the boy into that mess for? Nothing but a bunch of people sticking their noses in each other's business, telling people they're *sinning.*" Dad's nostrils had curled. "I've got no use for religion, myself. When Ben here's old enough, he can decide on his own what he thinks. Besides, how often do I get to see my kid?" He'd slurped from a mug of coffee laced heavily with milk and set it on the table with a bang. "You go on and do whatever it is they do at church. Us guys'll just hang here till you get back."

Ben still remembered the thrill he'd felt at the look Dad gave him across the table. Us guys. His father's carefree lifestyle as a sound mixer for a heavy metal band kept him on the road much of the time. When he wasn't traveling with the band, he rode with a motorcycle gang that rarely stayed in one place more than a couple of nights at a time. He showed up for unannounced visits with his son and the woman he'd never married only a few times a year. Ben cherished every precious moment of father-and-son time. If his idol thought church was a waste of time, it would have taken a two-ton tow truck to drag him to church after that.

When Mom returned home that day, Dad climbed on his motorcycle and left. Ben would never forget the final wave of his leather-clad arm and the way his long hair splayed out behind him in the wind as he zoomed down the street.

It was the last thing Ben ever saw of his father. Two weeks later, a state trooper came to their door to tell them he'd been killed in a motorcycle accident. Devastated and without another male role model, Ben held on to his father's memory by emulating his lifestyle—carefree and church free.

Brake lights flashed red on the car ahead of them. Ben slowed as the vehicle executed a left turn onto a residential street.

Beside him, Nikki watched him closely. "Am I right?"

It took a minute to remember what she was talking about. *Oh, yeah. Mérida.*

"Yeah," he admitted. "That's where I was thinking about going. But I still think you'd be better off staying in Miami while I take care of this. Don't get involved."

"I'm already involved, whether I want to be or not."

The set of her mouth, the way she jutted her chin forward and dared him to argue with her, stirred his memories. He never could win an argument with Nikki. Didn't look like that had changed. Besides being the most beautiful woman he'd ever met, she was still as stubborn as ever. Ben knew when it was time to give in and let her have her way.

"Fine. But don't hold me responsible if you get yourself in trouble."

Her mouth gaped open and her eyes went wide, as though he'd just said something shocking. After a few seconds, she closed her mouth and twisted around in the seat until she was facing the passenger window. He barely heard her whispered response.

"Don't worry. I won't."

At the softness in her tone, an unnamed emotion twisted in Ben's chest.

SEVEN

Their flight from Miami landed in Mexico City at 10:00 a.m. on Sunday morning. It would be about an hour or so before they could catch the connecting flight to Mérida, where they'd take the ferry the rest of the way to Cozumel. Nikki had spent nearly all her vacation cash to pay for her tickets. She didn't want to use a credit card in case someone was trying to track her whereabouts by watching her accounts. Probably a paranoid thought, but she didn't care. Ben, who didn't have a credit card, used his debit card. Easily traceable, but Nikki bit her tongue. He had no cash, and she didn't have enough to pay for both tickets.

They stepped off the airplane and into the bustle of the Mexico City airport. Even though they were inside, Nikki felt the familiar humidity in the air she drew into her lungs. She clutched Ben's arm when the people filing past them brushed against her. It was almost as crowded here as it had been at Mallory Square last night. It would be so easy to get separated.

Ben pressed her fingers with his other hand in what was probably supposed to be a comforting gesture, but he was busy scanning a board listing the departing flights.

"There it is." He pointed toward the board. "We've got to take the shuttle to terminal two. But first, I need to find a phone."

He set off with a confident step, alert but outwardly at ease. If Nikki hadn't felt the tension in the muscles of his arm, she would have thought he was nothing more than the American tourist he pretended to be. She forced what she hoped was a relaxed smile and matched his step.

"Who are you going to call?"

"Cesar." His glance flicked down at her, and she noted the worried lines at the corners of his mouth. "I hate to get him involved, but I can't think of anyone else I'd trust. We need a boat and equipment, and we need it quickly."

They spied a pay phone up ahead, and Ben strode toward it. Nikki stood beside him as he punched numbers on the keypad. She watched the people who passed, looking for a pair of familiar faces.

Don't be silly. The men from Key West weren't on our plane, and there were no other flights out of Miami this morning.

Still, mightn't the Reynosa cartel have airplanes at their disposal, even in Key West?

"Cesar. *Buenos dias,* my friend." Ben gave her a brief nod, and then began speaking quietly into the phone in rapid Spanish.

Nikki kept her eyes on the crowd. She didn't spot a single familiar face, thank goodness. Her gaze swept across the moving people.

A pair of dark eyes snagged hers. A man, standing in front of a newsstand not far away, was looking directly

at her. Their eyes met for a split second, and then he
looked away.

Heart thudding against her ribs, she watched him.
Latino, judging by the dark skin and jet-black hair, but
he was taller that the two in Key West. He appeared to
be inspecting the people who filed past, much as she had
done. But after a few seconds, his gaze strayed back in
her direction. Their eyes met once again. Nikki's pulse
kicked up another notch.

"Ben." She poked at his arm. "Ben, look over
there."

Ben kept the phone to his ear, but turned and looked
in the same direction. When he did, the man casually
stepped inside the newsstand. Ben looked at her, eyebrows drawn together in a question.

"He was watching us," she hissed.

After whispering a few more Spanish words into the
phone, he replaced the receiver. He studied the newsstand through narrowed eyes. "Are you sure?"

Nikki hesitated. Was she, or was she just being paranoid? "I think so."

"Then let's go while he's inside that store."

He placed a hand beneath her arm and pulled her
away. They blended into the crowd moving in the opposite direction. Nikki couldn't help glancing over her
shoulder, but she didn't catch sight of the man again.
Maybe she really was imagining things. Still, she
couldn't calm the uneasy feeling that fluttered in her
stomach.

The sun had long since passed its apex by the time
Ben and Nikki stepped off the ferry onto the dock in
San Miguel, Isla Cozumel's only town. Ben rested a hand

lightly on Nikki's back as they flowed with the crowd of tourists past the brightly colored buildings toward the town square. Mexican vendors called to them as they passed.

"*Buenos dias.* Best prices right here."

"Turquoise, *señor.* I make a good deal."

Ben refused with a brief smile, his gaze fixed ahead of him, though many of their fellow ferry passengers swarmed the covered wooden stalls with the enthusiasm of vacationing tourists with pockets full of money. He glanced at Nikki. She used to love dickering with the vendors, practicing her broken Spanish and making full use of her blond beauty to get the lowest price on whatever caught her fancy. Today she didn't spare them a glance.

As they approached the San Miguel square, a waving hand caught Ben's attention.

"There's Cesar." He pointed toward the curb, where his former boss stood in front of a dirty white Volkswagen Beetle.

They headed in that direction, and when they neared, Cesar wrapped Nikki in a quick hug. Ben nearly dropped his backpack in surprise. Though friendly, his former boss usually possessed more than his fair share of Mexican reserve and had never been much for outward displays of affection.

"*Señorita,* you are as beautiful as ever." White teeth gleamed in his broad face.

A becoming flush reddened Nikki's cheeks. "*Gracias,* Cesar. It's good to see you again."

He opened the passenger door and gestured for her to be seated. Nikki unshouldered the new backpack they'd purchased in the early morning hours at a twenty-four-hour Walmart in Miami and slid into the seat. When Cesar closed the door behind her, Ben followed him to the driver's side and ducked into the backseat. He moved to the center so he could see Cesar's profile as they drove.

As the vehicle pulled out into traffic, Ben planted his feet on either side of the rear floorboard and leaned forward. "Cesar, we can't thank you enough for this."

"*De nada,* my friend." He glanced into the rearview mirror. "Men have come asking questions about you."

Nikki threw a startled look at him over her shoulder. "They have?"

Cesar nodded. "Twice."

Ben winced. He had expected the Reynosa cartel would question his former employer and landlord. "I hope they didn't cause you any trouble."

Cesar shrugged. "I tell them what I know. You work for me three years. You live in my dive shop, watch over things for me at night. And when you leave, you don't tell me you are going."

Nikki turned in her seat. "You just left? Didn't even let him know you were leaving?"

Ben stiffened. Of all people, she was the one who had no business disapproving of his actions. After all, he'd taken his cue from her by leaving without a word to anyone. Only he had a good reason, and it wasn't just to avoid an unpleasant goodbye scene.

She must have realized what she was saying, because her face turned red in the instant before she twisted back around in her seat.

Cesar rushed to his defense. "No, no, it was right to leave quickly. If I know nothing, I can say nothing."

"That was my plan." A stab of guilt pushed Ben

backward in the seat. If the Reynosa people came back to question Cesar a third time, he wouldn't truthfully be able to deny any knowledge of Ben. He'd be forced to lie. And if he were caught lying to the most infamous drug cartel in Mexico, Ben hated to think what they would do to him.

"Cesar, I'm sorry I got you involved in this mess. If I'd had any other options, I would have taken them first."

The man's head dipped forward. "I know, amigo. Do not worry about me. I can take care of myself."

The Volkswagen stopped at a traffic light, then made an unexpected turn.

"We're not going to the dive shop?" asked Nikki before Ben could voice the question.

"No, to Puerto de Abrigo."

Ben nodded approval. Cesar wasn't taking any chances. It was one risk that had nagged at him since he made the call to Cesar when they changed planes in Mexico City. If the scuba shop was being watched, the Reynosa cartel would spot Ben and Nikki as soon as they arrived. All the care they'd taken by flying into Mérida and driving more than three hours to board the ferry at Playa would be for nothing. He shouldn't have worried. Cesar had foreseen the danger and moved the boat they were going to borrow to Puerto de Abrigo, the public marina.

The traffic slowed as they approached the entrance to the marina. Cesar pulled the Volkswagen over to the curb. He didn't get out of the car, but turned in his seat and gave them directions to the slip where the *Alexandra* was moored.

"Your equipment is in the storage chest." He raised an eyebrow at Ben. "You remember the combination?"

"Of course I do." Ben couldn't even count the number of small charter groups he'd taken out on the *Alexandra*.

"Leave the keys inside," Cesar instructed. "I will pick her up later." He paused. "Do you need a place to stay tonight?"

Gratitude washed over Ben at the generous offer. Cesar was putting himself in danger by offering them shelter. But if the Reynosa people were watching the dive shop, they were probably watching Cesar's home as well. Ben and Nikki couldn't take that chance.

He shook his head. "We'll find a place. You've done more than enough."

Nikki cracked open the door, then smiled a farewell. "Thank you, Cesar. I hope you don't get in any trouble because of us."

Cesar grinned. "I hope so, too, *señorita*."

She exited the car and tilted the seat forward for Ben. Before he left the vehicle, he clasped Cesar's shoulder. "I owe you, my friend."

His former boss dismissed the debt with a wave. "It is what friends do. Go with God." His gaze slid to Nikki. "Take care of her."

Ben glanced at the sidewalk, where she stood waiting, her new backpack slung over one shoulder. She would probably resist the idea that she needed taking care of. But he simply responded, "I will," and slid out of the car.

They stood watching, silent, as the Volkswagen pulled away from the curb and joined the line of traffic. The one drawback to the nomadic lifestyle Ben had chosen— the one his father had lived—was that friendships were hard to come by. Cozumel had been his home for longer than any other place since his mom died when he was nineteen. And Cesar was probably the best friend he'd ever had.

I sure hope I haven't brought trouble straight to his door.

The VW turned, and they lost sight of it. Ben scanned their immediate surroundings. Was anyone watching them? A line of taxicabs were parked along the sidewalk, waiting for tourists returning from daytime excursions. A few of the drivers stood outside their cars, chatting with one another as they waited. A man on a bicycle swept by, a mongrel-looking dog tucked in a metal basket strapped to the front handlebars. The cyclist didn't spare a glance in their direction as he passed. In fact, no one seemed to notice them at all, much less award them any undue attention. The weight on Ben's chest lightened slightly.

He unzipped the front pocket of his backpack and pulled out a pair of sunglasses. "Ready to go?" he asked Nikki.

She nodded, and they headed for the dock. Sailboat masts thrust high into the sky from boats in about half the slips. In front of them, turquoise waters glimmered in the afternoon sunlight. The color was a startling difference from the darker waters north of here, in Key West. He filled his lungs with salt-scented air, and instantly felt more alert. The reviving smell of the ocean was the same, regardless of the location.

"I'd forgotten how beautiful it is," Nikki said.

Ben glanced at her. A half smile hovered around her lips as she gazed across the water. Sunlight gleamed on her hair and highlighted her smooth skin with a healthy glow. A knot formed in his throat.

I'd forgotten how beautiful you are, he almost

said. He clamped his jaws shut before the words could slip out.

"This way."

His voice sounded gruffer than he intended. Nikki's eyebrows arched, but he increased his pace before she could say anything.

They found the *Alexandra* exactly where Cesar said it would be. The smaller of the two boats owned by his former employer's company, the thirty-four-foot *Alexandra* could accommodate twelve divers and was most often used for private charter groups. A red-and-white scuba flag flapped in a light breeze above the covered cabin.

Ben hopped from the dock into the boat and turned to offer Nikki a hand. She accepted his help, but released him the moment her feet touched the deck.

"Thank you," she murmured.

Ben crossed to the cabin door and dialed the sequence to release the combination lock. He descended the steps. Cesar had stowed all their equipment in the cabin—BCDs, masks, fins, regulators, weights and belts, and two tanks of air. The key was exactly where Cesar always kept it, in the lockbox stowed beneath one of the padded seats. Ben removed it, grabbed one of the tanks and climbed back to the deck.

"Our gear's down there." He slid the tank into a plastic holder and turned to Nikki. "Do you still remember how to hook up your equipment?"

An anxious expression stole over her features. "I think so."

"Good. If you can do that on the way, it'll save us some time." He glanced at his watch. "It's going to be close to four-thirty by the time we get there."

She lifted her head and looked toward the sun. "What time is sunset?"

"A little before six."

"And our plane doesn't leave until seven tomorrow night." Her voice wavered when she spoke, and she tucked a strand of hair behind her ear with a nervous gesture.

"That's right." She had balked at the late departure when they made the reservations, until he reminded her of the timing. They needed to wait at least twenty-four hours after diving before they flew, or risk decompression sickness. "Don't worry. We have plenty of time."

He smiled to calm her before ducking back into the cabin for the second tank. Though she'd lived with him for six months in one of the world's premiere scuba diving destinations, Nikki had never become a confident diver. Competent, but still overly cautious. She never grew to love the sport as he did. Many times he'd suspected the only reason she continued to dive was for him, to share in his passion. The last month before she left, she hadn't gone down at all.

I should have known something was wrong then. She fell out of love with diving first, then with me. Or was it the other way around?

He carried the second heavy canister out for her and slipped it into a holder. "You don't have to go down if you don't want to. I'm just going to descend, get the flash drive and come right back up."

For one moment, relief flooded her features. But then it fled, and the worry lines returned to her forehead. "No, that's all right. I'll go with you."

Does she still want to be with me?

The question washed onto the shores of his mind on

an accompanying wave of hope. But in the next instant, the hope was swept away, back out to sea.

Not a chance. She's done nothing but prove she wants to be rid of me from the moment we saw each other in Key West two days ago. She's going with me because she wants to keep an eye on me. She doesn't trust me.

The thought rankled.

He shrugged and turned away. "Suit yourself."

The inboard motor started right up, and the gas tank registered full. Good. They wouldn't have to waste time getting fuel. Ben intended to push the *Alexandra* to full throttle, get there as quickly as possible, retrieve the flash drive and get back to the shore. Then he could deposit Nikki in a hotel for the night.

Once she was out of his sight, maybe he'd be able to breathe freely again.

EIGHT

Nikki descended the narrow wooden steps into the cabin as Ben guided the boat out of the marina. During the months she lived in Cozumel, she dived off the *Alexandra* several times. A quick glance around the cabin showed nothing had changed. She stepped into the head with her backpack and pulled on the new swimsuit she'd purchased at Walmart last night, then slipped on a loose T-shirt over it.

A pair of BCDs—scuba diving vests, called Buoyancy Control Devices—hung on hooks over a wide cushioned bench in the cabin. She grabbed them, one small and the other large, and then draped the pair of octopus-looking regulators by the rubber hoses over her arm before heading back up.

When she stepped onto the deck, the boat was just clearing the marina. Ben pushed the throttle forward. Arms full, Nikki stumbled, struggling to maintain her balance. Ben leaned sideways and steadied her with an arm around her waist, the other hand still on the wheel.

"Careful."

His mouth was so close to her cheek his words were almost a caress. The strength of his arm sent ripples across her skin. Oh, that touch was so familiar! How easily she had once stepped inside the circle of this arm. A sudden longing for their old relationship washed over her and left her as unsteady as the moving deck beneath her feet. If she'd done things differently, if she'd told him about the baby, maybe he would have surprised her. Maybe…

She stiffened. No. She had made the right decision when she left Cozumel. If he had married her, it would have been from a sense of duty. He would have grown to hate both her and Joshua for robbing him of the lifestyle he loved.

"Sorry." She mumbled an apology as she stepped away from his steadying arm. She avoided looking at his face as she placed a BCD in front of each metal cylinder. "Haven't found my sea legs yet, I guess."

He didn't reply. The sound of the motor vied with the roar of the wind as the shore zoomed past on the port side. In the distance, off the starboard side, the mainland was a dark blur on the horizon. Salty spray from a big wave dotted her sunglasses, and she used the tail of her T-shirt to wipe it off.

It had been over two-and-a-half years since she assembled scuba equipment. Could she still remember how? She inspected the gear and found that everything was familiar. First, attach the BCD to the cylinder, then the regulator to the tank valve. Though she couldn't bring herself to look at Ben, she was intensely aware that he watched her every move. Well, that just made sense. Back when she had first met him, when she was a green newbie diver and he was her dive instructor, he'd described scuba gear as "your life support system in an alien environment." A mistake topside could become fatal sixty feet below the surface.

She positioned the regulator, which would allow them to breathe the compressed air in the tank, tightened the tank valve and attached the pressure inflator hose on the BCD, then stepped back to examine her work. "There. How's that?"

Ben lifted a shoulder. "Turn it on."

She picked up the pressure gauge and remembered to direct it away from her face as she twisted the knob on the tank. A slight hiss sounded for a second as air from the tank rushed through the regulator hoses. The procedure was coming back to her. The pressure gauge read a full 3000 psi, more than enough air for the quick dive they would be taking. She picked up the regulator second stage at the end of the long black hose and tested it by tapping the purge valve to make sure the mouthpiece was clear, and then taking a few breaths through it.

"This one's fine." She shouted to be heard over the noise of the boat's motor.

His eyebrows arched. "Did you check the secondary air source?"

A blush warmed her face, and she turned her back on Ben so he wouldn't see. So she'd forgotten one step. It had been almost three years, after all. She picked up the second regulator hose and breathed through the backup mouthpiece.

"Good. Now the other one."

His voice had taken on the tone of dive master, the undisputed person in charge on a dive. Instead of being irritated, Nikki's tension eased a fraction. If there was one thing Ben knew, it was scuba diving. She had never felt anything but entirely confident in his ability to keep her safe while diving. She needed that confidence now.

She moved to the second cylinder and followed the same procedure with the smaller BCD. When she twisted the knob to release air into the regulator, the pressure gauge needle sprang to life. But it didn't move nearly as far as she expected. She tapped the plastic cover with a finger, but the needle didn't budge.

"This one only has 1000 psi," she told Ben.

"Cesar must have mistakenly grabbed one that hasn't been refilled after the last dive." He lifted a shoulder, unconcerned. "It won't matter. We won't need near that much air. We're going to drop down and come right back up."

Nikki drew comfort from his nonchalant attitude. If Ben wasn't worried, then neither should she be.

Her task completed, she sat on the bench that lined the port side and watched the shoreline. Sandy beaches, hotels and resorts lined much of the southwestern side of the island, though the buildings grew less frequent the farther south they traveled. After a while, she saw nothing but the wild, dense bush that covered much of Cozumel.

She turned to shout a question for Ben. "Where are we going?"

"Maracaibo."

A stab of alarm tensed her muscles. She remembered that dive site. "The shallows?"

He shook his head. "The deep."

Maracaibo Deep. Dread formed a knot in her stomach. Maracaibo was the southernmost reef on the island, and one that only experienced divers attempted. The currents were strong, even for Cozumel. The reef formed a wall that *started* at ninety feet and dropped to depths beyond anything a diver could safely handle. Strong vertical currents could grab an unwary diver and sweep him—or her—down to his death in a matter of minutes. Nikki had never been there.

And she didn't want to start now.

Throughout the rest of the ride to the dive site, she remained silent. She couldn't have spoken if she wanted to. A rising panic clenched her throat and choked off any words she might have said.

NINE

The brilliance of the sun in the afternoon sky painted patterns on the turquoise water at the Maracaibo Deep dive site. Nikki flexed her knees and moved with the waves that rocked the *Alexandra* as she crossed the deck to don her scuba gear. The red-and-white scuba flag above her filled the silence between her and Ben with an irregular *flap-flap-flap* from the light breeze.

Instructions from her very first dive, delivered by the handsome dive instructor who would become her live-in boyfriend within the week, echoed from a distance of over two years. Nerves stretching taut with every step, she strapped on her weight belt, slid her feet into bright blue fins and sat on the bench to slip her arms into her BCD. She was still tightening the straps and checking the position of the regulator hoses when Ben finished gearing up.

"Here, let me help."

He heaved himself off the bench as though the heavy cylinder strapped to his back weighed only a few pounds. Not true, Nikki knew. The tank probably weighed close to forty pounds, about a third of her total body weight. She allowed Ben to grab the neck of her cylinder and help her stand.

"Thanks."

He let go, and the sudden weight dragged at her body. A moment to regain her balance, then she slowly made her way to the rear, shuffling her fin-clad feet across the deck to avoid tripping. She had almost reached the diving platform when Ben's voice stopped her.

"Hey, you forgot something."

He moved with ease, heedless of the fins that were so familiar to him they were almost an extension of his feet. An underwater light swung from a clip on one side of his BCD, his underwater camera on the other. In his hand he held her mask, the ribbed snorkel tube attached.

"Oh. Yeah." She gave a short, anxious laugh as she took it from him. "I, uh, think I'll need that."

His eyes bore into hers. "You're nervous." It was not a question.

A dozen excuses came to mind. An experts-only dive site. More than two years since her last dive. Less than a full tank of air. A little boy back in Portland who would be devastated if his mommy died in a tragic scuba accident and never came home.

But she didn't voice any of them, only nodded.

"You don't have to go." He laid a hand on her arm and smiled. "Really. I'll just drop down, grab it if it's still there and be right back up in a few minutes. You can wait for me here."

Oh, what a tempting offer! Nikki hesitated while a battle raged inside. She'd really like to do just that, wait here in the warm Mexican sunshine and let Ben retrieve the flash drive by himself. This was his mess, after all, not hers. Let him fix it by himself.

But the lessons he'd taught her years ago had been

well learned. She could still hear the vehemence in his voice as he insisted, "*Never* leave your dive buddy. Trouble can happen in an instant, and your dive buddy might be the only thing standing between you and death."

Nikki gulped. "No, that's okay. I—I want to."

He hesitated, then nodded. "Then whenever you're ready."

"Okay." Her voice shook with nerves. To distract him—or maybe to distract herself—she touched the camera clipped to his BCD. "So, are you planning on doing some sightseeing while we're there?"

He looked down, as though a little embarrassed. "Habit, I guess. You don't want to miss a Kodak moment."

Nikki felt the same way, though not about fish. Joshua did so many adorable things, she carried a camera with her all the time.

Thoughts of her son sent a wave of longing through her. "Let's just get down there and back up. No photo shoots this time."

She stepped to the edge of the platform, adjusted her mask and hesitated. The water here was as crystal clear as she remembered. Shadowy images looked like they might be only a few feet below the surface, but she knew that was an illusion. One reason Cozumel was considered such a great place for diving was the terrific visibility. Those shadows might be a hundred feet or more below her.

With the regulator mouthpiece between her clenched teeth, she placed a hand over her face so the force of impact didn't jerk off her mask and took a giant step off the platform. Salty water engulfed her in a cool embrace. She sank a few feet below the surface, but the air she'd put into her BCD turned it into a flotation device, and she popped back up almost immediately. Out of habit, she tapped the top of her head with a fist, the signal to the dive master that her entrance into the water was okay. Ben was beside her in the water a moment later.

He removed his mouthpiece and asked, "You ready?"

Nerves fluttered in her stomach. If she hadn't had a regulator in her mouth, she might have given in to the impulse to say *No! I've changed my mind*. Instead, she swallowed her fluttering nerves and nodded.

They faced each other, and Ben grasped her upper arm with one hand so the current wouldn't separate them as they descended. She held the release button on her BCD inflator at the same time he did. As the air deflated from her vest, Nikki slowly sank below the surface, the weights around her waist pulling her steadily downward. Her loud breath rasped through the regulator like Darth Vader. She could hear nothing else. She kept her gaze locked on Ben's face, his eyes clearly visible inside his mask.

The pressure squeezed inside her ears, and she pinched her nose shut and blew gently, as she'd been taught. The pressure equalized with a pop. She repeated the procedure every few seconds as they descended. After the first few times, she performed the task instinctively.

The world around them was tinged with blue. Light shafted through the water in visible rays, tiny sea particles dancing in the beams. Nikki glanced down. The dark structure below them grew larger as they neared and extended into the distance farther than she could see. The reef. The ocean pressed in on her from all sides, with no visible landmarks, nothing to connote their progress. Her sense of depth became fuzzy. How deep were they now? Her movements slowed by the water, she felt for the depth gauge at the end of one of her regulator hoses and held it up in front of her mask so she could read it. Fifty feet. Fifty-five. She equalized. Sixty.

This was as deep as she'd ever been, and they still hadn't reached the reef. The skin along her arms prickled with apprehension. The deeper the dive, the higher the pressure, the more nitrogen would be absorbed into her blood. The possibility of something going wrong increased exponentially. She stared into Ben's face. His lips formed a tight seal around the mouthpiece, but behind his mask, warm green-brown eyes peered into hers. His grip on her arm tightened, and the edges of his eyes crinkled in a smile.

He's done this lots of times. There's no need to worry.

The needle on the depth gauge continued to move. Sixty-five feet.

Seventy.

Seventy-five.

Nikki's breath came faster. She was aware of the fact only because she could hear it so well, a raucous panting that accompanied the thud of her heartbeat.

Relax. The faster you breathe, the more air you'll use.

And still, the needle on the depth gauge glided forward, like the second hand on a clock.

Eighty.

Eighty-five.

They finally reached the reef at ninety feet. Ben released her arm, held his two index fingers together, and pointed them in a direction parallel to the wall, a signal that they were to swim side by side. Nikki nodded, and kicked in that direction. Ben stayed right beside her.

They were swimming against a strong current, and she knew without checking her gauge that they were still descending. The pressure continued to build in her ears, and she continued to equalize as she swam.

A vertical shelf of living coral, the Maracaibo Wall was an intricate work of natural beauty. An infinite number of shapes and colors provided homes for hundreds of species of marine life. Sea anemone clung to the colorful coral, their flowerlike tentacles gyrating back and forth in the strong current. A school of yellow-striped fish floated by, and as Nikki admired the way they moved in unison, a flash of blue caught her eye. A queen angelfish swam regally past, just out of reach. So calm. So peaceful.

And still they descended.

One hundred.

One hundred five.

One hundred ten feet!

The dive tables she'd learned to read years ago came back to her. How much nitrogen had accumulated in her blood already? Panic sent her pulse into overdrive.

She grabbed at Ben's arm and, when he turned to face her, tapped on the depth gauge. Talking may not be possible at depth, but she poured her thoughts into her expression. She shook her head violently, which sent wisps of hair into wild floating acrobatics around the edges of her mask.

He responded by pointing. Right in front of them, recessed beneath an outcropping of coral, a dark opening yawned. A cave.

So that's where the flash drive is.

But if he thought she was going into a dark, scary cave at a hundred and ten feet, he had lost his mind. Nasty sea animals lived in caves, like sharks and moray eels. Plus, divers died in caves, even experienced ones. She stopped swimming, and within a few seconds the current had swept her back twenty feet in the direction they'd come. It was even stronger than she realized. Would she be swept away, never to be heard from again? She angled her body to face the current and kicked her fins against the flow just enough to stay in one place.

When Ben turned a questioning gaze her way, she shook her head again, even more violently.

He merely pointed again, turned and swam in that direction.

Indecision paralyzed her for an instant. But what else could she do? Surface on her own and swim back to the boat? Desert her dive buddy? She had no choice but to follow him.

But I'm not going in there. He knows I don't do caves.

She kicked against the current and caught up with him at the cave's entrance. Ben ran water-whitened fingers along the outcropping above the gaping black hole. Then he grabbed her hand and placed it on the ledge. His fingers folded hers around the coarse coral. When he held his flat palm in front of her face, relief washed through her.

He wants me to wait here for him.

She gripped the coral more tightly, anchoring herself against the strength of the current, and nodded.

Okay, I can do that. With her free hand, she tapped a finger against her wrist, where her watch would normally be. *Just don't be too long, okay? I don't want to have to come in there after you.*

A nod, and then he raised his own finger. He touched

it to his mouthpiece, and then to hers. An underwater kiss. They had come up with the gesture during their very first dive together, a way to share an intimate underwater moment even in the midst of a dozen other divers.

Nikki sucked a deep breath through her regulator. What did he mean by that? Ben's eyes widened, and for a moment, he looked as startled as she felt.

Then he turned gracefully upside down and kicked his fins. At the cave's entrance, he unclipped the dive light from his BCD and flipped it on. With the light held in front of him, he swam into the cave headfirst and disappeared from view.

Nikki clung to the coral and stared out into the blue depths on three sides. She raised her hand and rubbed her fingers across her regulator where Ben had brushed his kiss a moment before. Obviously, he hadn't meant that as a real kiss. It was a gesture made without thought, something they used to do back when they were in love. A habit. It didn't mean anything.

A pair of grouper swam by and a school of fish that looked like Dory in *Finding Nemo*. Above her, a flash of silver drew her attention, and she looked up. A long, thin fish with a distinctive underbite came into view. A barracuda. Instinctively, she felt for the cross that normally hung at her neck, but then remembered she had left it on the boat. A good thing. Barracudas were attracted to shiny objects. Nothing she wore should attract his attention. The fish started to swim past, then, in a heart-stopping moment, turned in her direction.

Before she had a chance to panic, Ben emerged from the cave. Startled, the barracuda veered away and disappeared into the limitless blue ocean in front of her. Nikki relaxed her death grip on the coral.

Unaware that he'd just interrupted a potentially frightening encounter, Ben held his dive light out toward her. The light had gone out.

Oh, no. The battery died or something, so he can't see to get the flash drive.

Wait a minute. He held a second light in his other hand, the bulb still illuminated. Two dive lights, when he'd only taken one into the cave.

He must have hidden the flash drive inside the other light.

A great idea, actually. A dive light was waterproof and designed to withstand pressure. He must have tucked the drive inside, and then wedged it somewhere in that cave. The perfect hiding place.

She released her coral handhold and clapped her hands. *Well done, Ben.*

Smile creases appeared at the corners of his eyes. When he had clipped both lights to his BCD, he gave her a thumbs-up, the signal to ascend.

And boy, was she ready!

Their return trip required little effort. All they had to do was let the current sweep them along and make sure they didn't ascend too quickly. Nikki was content to follow Ben's lead. That was another thing she'd always admired when diving with Ben—he was always oriented and knew the exact location of the boat, while she frequently became disoriented underwater.

At fifty feet, Ben placed three fingers of one hand beneath the palm of the other, the diver's signal that it was time for a safety stop. They hovered in the water, holding on to each other's BCDs to stay together, while

Nikki tried not to imagine the nitrogen dissipating from her blood. After three minutes, Ben nodded, and they continued their ascent.

At fifteen feet, they stopped again for their second and final safety stop. The surface looked close enough to reach up through the crystal clear water and plunge a hand into the sun-warmed air. The hull of the *Alexandra* was a dark, oblong shape overhead. Nikki saw that the sun had dropped closer to the horizon. What time was it? She took hold of Ben's wrist and twisted it so she could see his watch. Almost five o'clock. They'd only been in the water fifteen minutes, though it had seemed like hours.

A sound interrupted her raspy breathing. A low hum, distant but growing louder. She turned a silent question toward Ben and saw that he had heard it, too. His head tilted back as he scanned the surface above them. Then he pointed.

Another dark oblong approached. A boat. Only two-thirds the size of the *Alexandra,* which meant it was probably a private vessel.

Nikki's heartbeat pounded in her ears.

It could be anyone, she reasoned. *Scuba divers getting ready for a night dive, maybe. This is a public dive site, after all.*

She searched Ben's eyes for reassurance but found none. Instead, his forehead above the mask held deep creases.

He's worried.

And that realization made *her* worried. The hum of the boat's motor grew softer as the dark shadow slowed, and then came to a stop above them.

Right beside the *Alexandra.*

TEN

Aware that Nikki was watching him, Ben forced himself to remain calm. He had no doubts at all that the arrival of the second boat meant trouble. Their scuba flag indicated to everyone that there were divers in this area, and the speed of the approach displayed a sloppy lack of concern for the safety of anyone in the water. Plus, that boat didn't simply stop near the *Alexandra*, it came directly alongside her. The two hulls were side by side, nearly touching. Which probably meant the *Alexandra* was being boarded right now.

He considered their options. They could go back down, leave the area, then surface and swim toward the island. No, bad idea. The island was several miles away, and Nikki wasn't a strong surface swimmer. They'd never make it, certainly not before sunset. And of course they wouldn't be able to signal for help—the flares were onboard.

They could...

He grappled for another idea and came up empty.

A watery figure appeared above them. A man stepped onto the dive platform of the *Alexandra*, his image unfocused but unmistakable through the clear water. He leaned over and peered down, toward them.

If Ben could see him, no question about whether he could see them. Nikki looked up, and then locked a wide, blue-eyed gaze onto Ben.

He lifted both hands, palms up. *What choice do we have?*

With a thumbs-up, he gave the signal to surface.

A few kicks of their fins took them into the air. Ben spat out the regulator and ripped the mask off his face so he could see their situation clearly. Nikki hung close to his side, clutching his arm just below the water's surface.

The Mexican man on the dive platform stood with his feet spaced apart, his body moving easily with the motion of the rocking boat. Waves had wet the cuffs of his dark trousers, and the setting sun reflected off his white, short-sleeved shirt. Jet-black hair slicked back from a high forehead, caught in a tight ponytail at the base of his skull. He looked familiar, and in a flash Ben realized why. This was the man who had been watching them in the Mexico City airport. He lifted a cigarette to his lips, and the wind wisped the smoke away the moment it left his mouth.

If Ben swam over to the platform, he could reach up, grab one of his ankles and have the guy in the water before he knew what had happened to him. Once in the water, Ben thought he could take him.

Except for what he saw in the second boat.

It had been tied off to the *Alexandra,* and three men stood on the open deck. Young, muscular, not a single smile between them. All three seemed to tower over them and stared with menacing glares into the water at him and Nikki. All three clutched assault rifles in their hands.

Nikki's fingers bit into Ben's arm.

The first man, obviously the boss, drew again on the cigarette, then spoke in heavily accented English. "We have come to retrieve the information."

A dangerous glint in the leader's dark eyes, evident even from this distance, told Ben this was not a man to be toyed with. And yet, the flash drive was their only bargaining chip. He needed to play his advantage for everything it was worth.

He forced a laugh. "Yeah, us too. But it's gone."

The man's expression did not change. "Gone?" His tone clearly announced that he didn't buy the story for a minute.

Still, Ben had to try. "When I stashed it in that cave, I tried to wedge it tight, but—" He shrugged. "The current here's really strong, you know?"

Dark eyes studied him for a long moment and then glanced toward one of the men in the other boat. Not a word of command was spoken, but the second man lowered his weapon. In the next instant, a series of loud reports cracked in the air. The water a foot away from them erupted with bullets.

Nikki threw her arms around Ben, clearly terrified, and a short shriek escaped her lips.

"Hey! What was that for?" Ben shouted. "I can't give you something I don't have."

The man on the *Alexandra* took another calm draw on his cigarette. "I don't believe you."

"Well, I can't help that, can I?" A note of belligerence crept into Ben's voice.

Nikki's grip on him tightened. She whispered, her voice low enough that only he could hear, "Give it to them."

He whispered back, "I thought you wanted to give it to the feds?"

"I'd rather stay alive." She heaved a ragged breath and dropped her forehead to his shoulder.

Ponytail Guy spoke again. "Perhaps if you don't know where to find the drive, the pretty *señorita* has something to share with us."

A deep laugh drew Ben's attention to the trio on the other boat. The one in the center leered at Nikki. "I will get her," he called to his boss. He laid his weapon down and started to peel off his shirt.

All the horrible things they might do to Nikki if they got hold of her flashed into his mind. Fear marched across his flesh, raising bumps in its wake. Apparently the same ideas occurred to Nikki, for she whimpered in his ear.

Ben looked back at Ponytail. "All right, you win. Give me your word that you'll leave her alone, that you won't harm either of us, and I'll give you the device."

White teeth flashed in the brown face. "You ask for my word? What makes you think I would keep it?"

His throat was so dry Ben barely managed to reply. "I figure even a drug dealer has enough pride to honor a bargain."

The man's head dipped forward in a mock bow. "I am touched by your trust. You have my word we will not touch you or the girl." When he raised his head, his dark eyes glittered dangerously. "Now, give me the data."

With slow movements, Ben unclipped the dive light from his BCD. Finding it had been something of a miracle, since he'd become convinced that the current had probably washed it away over the past several months. The thought had also occurred to him that another experienced diver might explore that cave, discover the crevice where he'd wedged it. But no, he found it in exactly the same place he had left it.

He raised the light out of the water and threw it football style. Ponytail snatched it out of the air. Cigarette dangling from his lips, he twisted off the head and tossed the bulb section into the water, then peered into the battery compartment.

"Very smart." He commended Ben's ingenuity with a half nod, then pulled the waterproof pouch from inside. The rest of the dive light followed the bulb section, and Ponytail flattened the vinyl bag. Ben caught sight of the black rectangle, no longer than his thumb, inside.

With a flick, the cigarette went flying into the waves. Ponytail turned and stepped from the dive platform onto the *Alexandra*'s deck, headed for the helm. A moment later, the motor revved to life. So did the second boat's.

"Hey, wait a minute." Ben gave his shout enough volume to be heard over the roar of two motors. "What are you doing? You can't just leave us here. It's too far to swim back to shore."

The sound of the motor almost stole the man's laughter. "Don't worry. You won't be swimming."

That's when Ben noticed the activity on the second boat. The men had put down their weapons. One untied the ropes that held the two boats together, while the other two bent to pick up...

Buckets?

Horror stole over him as he guessed the contents.

"No, wait!" Panic made his voice high, but he couldn't help it. "We trusted you. You gave your word."

Ponytail turned from the helm and slapped a hand

to his chest. "I kept my word. I left her alone. I will not touch either of you."

The water churned as he pushed the throttle forward, and the *Alexandra* sped away. Nikki turned toward him, fear warring with the questions on her face.

"He's just going to leave us here, in the middle of the ocean?" Terrified tears choked her words.

At that moment, the two men tipped their buckets overboard. The contents splashed into the water, staining it red with blood. Chunks of fish guts and mangled flesh littered the surface. A second later, two more buckets full of chum followed.

Without a backward glance, the men sped away in the wake of the *Alexandra*, leaving Ben and Nikki alone in what would soon be shark-infested waters.

ELEVEN

"**I**s that *blood?*"

Her voice ended in a shriek, but Nikki didn't care. She clutched at Ben as a wave brought the ominous red stain closer.

"Fish blood." Ben sounded amazingly calm, though Nikki felt the tension in the muscles beneath her grip. "Not human blood."

The ocean swelled with a huge wave. They rose on it, then dipped back down the other side, bobbing like corks on the surface.

"I don't care what kind of blood it is." She tried not to shout, she really did, but a full-fledged panic attack had her in its grips. "They just baited the water for sharks, didn't they? We've got to get out of here!"

She released him and started swimming. Her fins, fueled by a jolt of adrenaline, propelled her through the water at a speed much faster than she could have managed on her own. Or maybe her kicks were fueled by fear. Whatever. As long as she got out of here before the sharks arrived, that was all that mattered. On her fifth stroke, Ben caught up with her.

"Nikki, stop." He grabbed her BCD and jerked her

toward him. "It's no use. We can't outrun them. Look there."

They rose on another swell, and when she was at the top, Nikki looked in the direction he indicated. In the distance—but not nearly far enough—an eerie triangular fin broke the surface. And it was coming this way.

A scream rose in her throat, but she choked it off. "We've got to get out of here!" She twisted to break Ben's grip on her BCD, but he held fast.

"Listen to me." He maneuvered himself around so their faces were inches apart. "More people die from dog attacks every year than sharks. You know that. You've heard me say it a thousand times."

"Yes, but that was—" She bit off her words. She'd been about to say, *That was before. I have a child to take care of. Things are different now.* She gulped in a breath. "You can't be seriously suggesting that we hang around here. I don't think these sharks know the statistics, Ben."

"No, I'm not suggesting that." His reasonable tone sounded in sharp contrast to her sarcasm. "But panicking is the worst thing we can do. They can sense that. The second worst thing we can do is make a bunch of noise swimming away. A lot of splashing on the surface is going to look like injured prey to a shark."

One part of her mind recognized his logic and the fact that he appeared to be calm—on the outside, anyway.

She tried to mimic him. "So, what do you suggest?"

"We go back down. Sharks don't recognize scuba divers as prey. The bubbles confuse them. We'll be safer if we can get under them. As soon as they've eaten all the chunks, they'll realize there's no more food in this area, and they'll leave."

"But...but..." A thousand facts crowded together in her mind. When she had first started diving, she'd learned to read the dive tables that specified how long a diver had to wait between dives before it was safe to resubmerge. The surface time allowed the nitrogen to dissipate from blood and tissue. How long were they supposed to wait after a one-hundred-ten-foot dive? Certainly longer than the five minutes they'd been on the surface. The results of ignoring that wait time were unthinkable. Nitrogen narcosis. Air embolism, which would kill them. The bends, which could also be deadly.

And yet, the alternative—she gulped—was equally deadly. Becoming dinner for a school of blood-crazed sharks.

The tide had swept the blood away from them, or maybe the blood had diluted in the water. Either way, Nikki could no longer see the red stain. But she could still locate several large chunks of chum, floating on the surface about fifty feet away. An ominous fin broke the surface just beyond, and in the next instant—an eruption of water, a flash of razor-sharp teeth, a violent splash and the chum was gone.

She couldn't help it. She screamed.

"Nikki." Ben shouted in her ear. "We're going. Now!"

He grabbed her regulator, shoved it in her mouth and jerked down the mask off her forehead over her eyes. Terror blazed through her brain, pushing coherent thought beyond reach. All she could do was cling to Ben. And obey him. He slapped the BCD valve into her hand, and she pushed the button. Air hissed out of her vest, and water crept up her mask as she sank.

Silence pressed against her ears, trapping her alone inside her body with a fear that gnawed at her mind. Then she remembered to breathe, and the rasp of air surging through her regulator gave her an audible focal point.

Breathe in. Breathe out. Keep a constant stream of bubbles.

Pressure squeezed her ears. She pinched her nose and blew, her gaze never leaving Ben's eyes framed inside his mask.

A movement just behind her, at the edge of her peripheral vision. She turned her head.

And screamed through her regulator.

A huge shark passed not four feet away from them. Snout short and bluntly rounded. Pectoral fins large and narrow. Two sets of dorsals. And small, round, dead-black eyes that seemed to catch her in its stare.

Ben crushed her arms in his grip. She forced herself to look away from the predator, back at him, as they continued to descend. Out of the corner of her eye, she saw the shark turn and head for the surface. Terrified tears blurred her vision. They filled her eyes and dripped down her face to pool on the rubber seal of her mask.

God, we need help! Please, don't let us die here.

Ben released one of her arms. His hand rose to cup the back of her head, and he leaned forward to rest his mask against hers. She could almost hear his thoughts, could almost feel the comfort he so obviously was trying to give her.

Ben knows what he's doing, she reminded herself. *I*

can't panic. Sharks can sense panic, remember? I just have to trust him.

A sob choked her. *Oh, Joshua, I didn't trust your daddy enough to tell him about you. But I have to trust him now, or I'll never see you again.*

She drew a deep breath into her lungs, and—

Nothing happened.

She sucked in again, but the Darth Vader rasp did not occur.

With frenzied movements, she scrabbled for her pressure gauge and held it to her face.

Her tank was empty. She had run out of air.

The stream of bubbles from Nikki's regulator ceased. Ben had been expecting it. Her tank had been low to begin with. Plus, she'd been anxious on the way down to the wall, and an anxious diver sucked air at a much faster rate than a calm one. Behind her mask, her eyes grew round as basketballs. Hysteria swelled her pupils until they were almost as black as the shark's.

Acting quickly, before she could shoot to the surface in a panic, Ben unclipped the secondary air source from his BCD and held it up in front of her. She clutched at it, and in a single motion, jerked her regulator out of her mouth and replaced it with his spare. Ben tapped on the face of his own regulator, the signal to "relax and breathe," but he doubted if she remembered. So he held her gaze with his, willing her to calm down. If she kept sucking air like that, she'd hyperventilate, and that would be disaster at sixty feet.

After a few gasps, the rate of her breathing slowed. She gave a shaky nod, and then lifted her hand. Her fingers formed the "okay" signal.

Good. Now Ben had to figure out what to do. His air pressure gauge registered almost 2000 psi left in the cylinder, which wouldn't last long with two of them breathing on it. He looked up and counted the ominous dark figures circling above them. Three nurse sharks, which were not a threat. In fact, he was surprised they stirred themselves from the bottom, where they habitually rested. A hammerhead, too, which normally would have thrilled him, because sightings in this area were so rare.

And the Caribbean reef shark. He'd spotted it at the surface, which is what prompted him to descend so quickly. This one was at least six feet long, big enough to make anybody sit up and take notice. Caribbean reef sharks were bold and had been known to make close passes at divers, like this guy had done a minute ago. They could be persistent when provoked by chumming, and had been known to attack. Good thing Nikki didn't know enough about sharks to identify that fellow.

He looked around to get his bearings. The water had darkened as the sun sank in the sky, and he could no longer see the location of the wall. That *might* be the outline there, forty feet below them, but it was hard to tell with no light. Still, they couldn't go down to be certain, not with their limited air supply. The only other choice was to surface, which wasn't an option at the moment. He gave Nikki the signal to start swimming, and indicated the direction.

He locked his arm through hers and pulled her close so there was no danger that the current would separate them and rip the regulator out of her mouth. The trembling in her arm provided clear evidence that she had not yet conquered her terror. Well, who could blame her?

They'd just encountered four members of the most infamous drug cartel in all of Mexico, which, in his opinion, was a far more deadly danger than a few sharks.

Their situation was dire. They had no identification, no money, nothing. They were stranded in Mexico. And they'd lost Cesar's boat. He winced. What would Cesar think when he realized they weren't returning with the *Alexandra?* That boat was his livelihood, a vital part of his business. Would he think his friends had stolen it? No, Cesar knew the Reynosa cartel was after them. He'd surmise what had happened. He'd have no choice but to go to the police, but he wouldn't point a finger at Reynosa. To do so would be suicide. No, he'd report the boat stolen, and he'd be forced to name Ben as the thief.

Of course, it wouldn't make any difference. They probably wouldn't make it to shore, anyway. It was a long, long swim against a powerful and unpredictable current, and the sunlight was almost gone. The chances that they'd survive were slim.

Ben kept a close watch on the air gauge. When it reached 500 psi, he angled them toward the surface. They stayed at fifteen feet for the required three minutes, but he didn't stop their forward motion. Easier to make progress underwater, even with the current, than to fight the waves at the surface. Finally, when he was certain it was safe, he gave Nikki the thumbs-up.

They dropped their weight belts and popped to the surface.

Nikki ripped her mask off her face and erupted into tears.

"Hey, calm down. Come here."

In the next moment, he almost submerged again when

she threw her arms around him. Her cold cheek pressed against his, and sobs filled his ear. The bulky BCDs made the embrace awkward, but he held her as tightly as he could, stroking her wet hair and soothing her with, "It's okay. You're safe now."

Yeah, not true at all, but what else could he say?

Nikki didn't buy the lie. She jerked backward enough to look him in the face. Her fingers gripped the shoulders of his BCD. "I'm *not* safe! How can you say that? I'm floating out here in the middle of the ocean—" a sob "—with sharks—" another sob "—and it's getting dark." The shakes with which she punctuated her words threatened to dunk him under. "So don't lie to me, Ben."

"Sorry. What do you want me to say?"

"I don't know!" Her volume rose to a shout. "I want you to tell me how we're going to get out of this. I want you to come up with a plan."

She was working herself into a frenzy. In another minute, she'd start striking out, like a panicked swimmer, and drown them both.

"I want you to figure out how we're going to—"

Ben stopped her the only way he knew how. He jerked her forward and covered her mouth with his.

Warmth chased away the ocean's chill as Nikki's lips softened beneath Ben's kiss. Oh, how she remembered this giddy feeling, this delicious—

She jerked backward. *What am I doing?*

"I…I'm…" She shook her head to clear it. "Why did you do that?"

"You were getting hysterical." A grin crooked his lips sideways. "I couldn't think of a better way to shut you up."

Oh, the feelings that washed over her at the sight of that crooked smile. The strength of them took her by surprise.

I'm still in love with him.

The fact struck her with tidal wave force. No. That couldn't be. She had feelings for him, sure. That was natural, because he was the only man with whom she'd ever been…intimate. The first time she laid eyes on Ben Dearinger, she had fallen head-over-heels, throw-common-sense-to-the-wind, crazy in love with him. She had walked away from her stable life, her job, her goals, even her family, because she had been swept away by the strength of her feelings for him. They'd lived together, created a child together. Whether he knew it or not, there would always be a connection between them, but she had gotten over her infatuation with him years ago. She didn't *love* him.

But no matter how hard she tried to convince herself, the truth tolled like a bell in her mind and resonated through every cell of her being. She loved him. She loved Ben Dearinger.

No. I will not *allow myself to be snared by his magnetism again. I have commitments now that I didn't have before—to Joshua and to God.*

Her thoughts grasped on to the reminder like a lifeline. She belonged to God now. He had saved her soul when she wandered into the little mission church on the island almost three years ago, pregnant and frightened about her uncertain future. Could He save her life now?

Oh, God! Help me. Please rescue me.

Whether she was praying for rescue from the ocean

or from her feelings, she didn't know. She focused her tumultuous thoughts into prayers, silent pleas to the One who was powerful enough to handle any situation, even this one.

"Nikki?"

She opened her eyes to find Ben watching her, his eyebrows scrunched together with growing alarm. Nikki realized her lips were moving with unvoiced prayers. She must look like a crazy woman.

"Pray with me, Ben. We have to pray, ask God to rescue us."

His jaw twisted sideways. "Come on, Nikki. You know that's not going to do any good."

"What if you're wrong?" Salty water splashed into her face as she hooked her fingers into the sleeves of his vest and pulled him forward. "What if God really does hear our prayers, Ben? Have you ever thought of that?"

His lips formed a tight line of disgust. "You know how I feel about all that church stuff."

"I don't care how you *feel* about it," she shouted into his face. "I want to pray."

He matched her volume. "Fine, go ahead. I'm not stopping you."

Thick, wet locks of hair slapped her face as she shook her head. "The Bible says if two people agree in prayer, God will do it. You have to pray with me."

His eyes swept upward, toward the swiftly darkening sky. "Oh, come on. You haven't really bought into that garbage, have you?"

"Pray with me, Ben. Please!" Tears blurred her vision. She clenched her eyes shut and struggled against deep sobs that came out as choking gasps of air. When she opened her eyes, Ben was watching her with increasing alarm.

"Okay, Nikki." He released a deep breath. "If you want to pray, I will. Just don't get hysterical, okay? We've got to keep a level head."

Her chest shuddered as she nodded. He only agreed to humor her, but she didn't care. "Thank you."

"So, uh, how do we, you know, do it?" He glanced around, as though looking for an instruction manual to float by. "What do we say?"

"I'll talk." Nikki drew in a deep breath, past the knot in her throat, into lungs that couldn't be tighter if her chest was being squeezed in the jaws of a whale. "Just close your eyes and listen, and say Amen when I finish."

She watched to make sure Ben obeyed. Hysterical laughter simmered in the bottom of her throat when he closed his eyes. Nikki felt it and knew she couldn't let it out or she'd never be able to stop. Instead, she closed her own eyes and poured her thoughts heavenward.

"Dear Lord, we're in a mess, and we need Your help. Please don't let us die. Keep the sharks away from us, and send somebody to help. The coast guard, maybe, or some night divers or somebody. Anybody. Just, please, get us out of here. In Jesus's name, Amen."

"Amen." Ben's response rang with obedience more than reverence. "Do you feel better?"

Oddly, she did. A comforting sense of peace dulled the sharp edges of the panic that gripped her. She managed a trembling smile and nodded.

"Well, good. At least one of us does." His voice, laced

with sarcasm, sliced into the air between them. "Now that we got that out of the way, maybe we can put our heads together and come up with a *real* plan to—"

His words cut off abruptly. Jaw dangling open, Ben's gaze focused on something behind her. A jolt of fear electrified her nerves. Had the sharks followed them? She turned, expecting to see a sinister fin heading in their direction. Instead, she saw—

A boat.

Running lights illuminated a swath in front of the boat, and the stern light glowed like a beacon above the dark waters through which the boat sped. The hum of the motor reached her an instant later.

"Help!" Nikki raised her arms and waved, screaming at full volume. "We need help."

Ben's voice joined hers. "Hey, we're over here!"

She kicked her fins with frantic movement, and propelled herself upward in the water several feet, shouting the entire time. Beside her, Ben unclipped his flashlight from his BCD and turned it on. He aimed the beam at the boat and waved it back and forth.

The signal worked. The volume of the motor decreased and the boat slowed. Nikki increased her frenetic waving and pushed her voice to decibels she'd never attained before.

A voice came to them across the water from the boat's speaker. "*Nadadores, te vemos. Estomos vinlendo ayudar.*"

Nikki had no idea what the Spanish words meant, but Ben's laughter echoed across the water's surface. "They see us. They're coming to help."

He continued to wave the light as the boat executed a turn in their direction.

Nikki's sobs formed words. "Thank You, God. Thank You."

TWELVE

Ben shivered inside his wrapping of towels and looked at the faces around him. Their rescue boat was a privately chartered deep sea fishing vessel, heading in to shore an hour behind schedule. When he caught sight of the boat, coming so quickly after their prayer, a shiver had swept through his body. A shiver that had nothing at all to do with the temperature of the water. He hadn't prayed since he was nineteen, when he had begged God to save his mother from cancer. He had not set foot in a church since that day when he was ten and he learned his father's views on religion, but as he sat beside the hospital bed, he'd made a promise that if God would save Mom, he would start going. That was a promise he didn't have to keep.

And yet, Nikki prayed, and a boat showed up to rescue them within seconds. He'd half expected to find it filled with priests or missionaries or something.

"I'm telling you, folks, you shoulda seen that fish." The big man wearing a Kentucky Wildcats cap, who definitely wasn't a priest, spread his hands as far apart as they would go. "I never saw nothing like that in the crick back home. Fought like the wildcat on this here cap, too. Snapped the line just when I was about to get him close enough to net. Hey, Ed, you got pictures on that camera of yours, didn't you? Show the folks."

"Ralph, they don't want to hear about your fish." Thankfully, Ed, red faced from too much sun and not enough sunscreen, didn't produce his camera. "They been through a terrible ordeal."

Manuel, the men's fishing guide, held a white plastic cup beneath the spigot on the water cooler and refilled it. He handed the cup to Nikki, who downed it for the third time. Wrapped in a couple of towels of her own, her violent shaking had finally calmed to an occasional tremble.

Ben drained his own cup. They were both probably dehydrated from their extended time breathing the extra-dry compressed air under water. When Manuel handed him another cupful, he mumbled, *"Gracias,"* without looking the man in the face. That Manuel disapproved of his request to not contact the Mexican water patrol was obvious. Censure oozed from the man's pores and the tightly clamped line of his mouth.

Thankfully, the boat's captain had listened to reason. In a whispered conversation in Spanish, while the Kentucky fishermen attended to Nikki, Ben claimed that he and a group of fellow tourists had rented a boat to do some scuba diving on their own. Between too much beer, the hot sun and too little food, things had gotten a bit wild. They'd been left behind, apparently forgotten. But he didn't want to get his friends in trouble by contacting the police. The captain's shrewd eyes had pierced into him as he talked, and Ben knew he suspected there was far more to the story than he was being told.

Most business owners, especially those who made their living from the tourist trade, would have followed the rules and notified the authorities, regardless of the request not to. Whether this captain disliked the police, or he took pity on what he assumed were a couple of traumatized tourists, Ben didn't know, but he had agreed to return them to the marina without getting the authorities involved.

Yet another reason for Ben to wonder if this particular boat coming across them at exactly the right moment was, indeed, a coincidence.

The *policía* would ask far too many questions that Ben wasn't in a position to answer right now, not to mention the fact that he had no identification and no money. Plus, he'd just as soon not advertise the fact that they'd survived. As long as the Reynosa cartel thought them dead, they were safe.

Nikki leaned sideways against him. Her lips were still blue with cold, but a touch of color had begun to return to her cheeks. "We made it." She closed her eyes and rested her head on his shoulder.

We're out of the ocean, but we're not out of deep water yet.

He clamped his mouth shut on the words. When the direness of their situation hit her, she would probably insist they pray again.

The private fishing charter operated out of Puerto de Abrigo, the same marina where Cesar had left the *Alexandra* for them. By the time they docked, full darkness had fallen. Lights illuminated the marina and the string of boats that lined the mooring docks. Ben shed his damp towels to help a surly Manuel secure the boat, then as the Kentuckians gathered their belongings, hefted their gear up on the dock. Nikki collected the fins and masks and accepted the captain's assistance in climbing onto the dock.

"You are sure I cannot take you to your hotel? I have a car." The gaze he turned toward Ben held suspicions, but they remained unspoken.

Only if you want to foot the tab, too, since all our money is gone.

"No, we'll be fine." Ben put on a guileless smile. "We don't want to inconvenience you any more than we already have."

"We can't thank you enough." Nikki placed a free hand on the man's brown arm. "You were an answer to prayer."

Normally, that comment would have evicted a disagreement from Ben, or at the very least, an eye roll. At the moment, though, he couldn't bring himself to do either. Instead, he bid farewell to Ed and Ralph, hefted the BCDs with their attached cylinders, one in each hand, and headed down the dock.

Nikki fell in beside him. "Where are we going?"

He glanced behind them to be sure their rescuers were out of earshot. "First, I'm going to ditch this stuff somewhere. It's too heavy to lug around."

"I hate to throw away Cesar's equipment. He'll have to replace it, won't he?"

A blast of laughter escaped before he could stop it. He turned an incredulous stare on her. "You're kidding, right? He has to replace a *boat,* Nikki. A couple of BCDs are nothing compared to that."

She nodded but didn't reply. A wooden plank creaked beneath their bare feet, which otherwise made no sound at all. Nikki's feet were dainty, half the size of his, with ten bright pink toenails. As they passed the slip where the *Alexandra* had been docked, Ben cast a regretful glance into the empty space. The marina was even more deserted than when they'd left, with only a few people cleaning up after a day at sea and readying their boats for the night. They drew a couple of curious stares. At least they'd both chosen to wear T-shirts beneath their BCDs, though they looked pretty awful at the moment, wrinkled and stiff with dried salt. Still, they would have drawn even more attention strolling through the marina wearing nothing but bathing suits.

As they walked, Ben scouted around for a place to stash the equipment. A healthy-looking bush just inside the entrance looked like a good prospect. He stopped, set the cylinders down and unclipped his underwater camera from the BCD. Good thing he'd thought to bring it, because it was the only thing they owned at the moment. Maybe he could hock it for enough money to…what? He hadn't thought that far ahead.

The waterproof case was too bulky, though. He unfastened it, buttoned the digital camera inside the pocket of his now-dry swim trunks, then stooped to shove everything beneath the bush.

He gestured for Nikki to hand him the fins and masks, and stored them with the rest. "We'll call Cesar and tell him where to find them. And explain what happened to his boat."

Nikki winced. "I hope his insurance covers theft."

"I'm sure it does." Ben gave the gear a final shove to push it farther beneath the foliage, then straightened.

"Now what?" she asked.

He searched her face for signs of the panic she had exhibited earlier. Her skin was still pale. Creases at the corner of her eyes whitened with strain, but she appeared to be calm. Trusting, even. The look she turned on him stirred unusual feelings deep inside, feelings of responsibility and protectiveness.

They pressed on him like a weight. Could he come through for her? He was fresh out of ideas.

Think. We've lost our passports, our money, everything. Who helps tourists when their stuff gets stolen?

When the answer came to him, he slapped his forehead. "Duh! The American Consulate. There's an extension office in Cozumel."

Relief smoothed the creases around her eyes. "Won't it be closed?"

"Yeah, but maybe they'll have an emergency number or something. We've got to find a telephone."

He put an arm around her waist to guide her back in the direction they came, toward the marina office. When they fell in step beside each other, he didn't remove his arm. Nor did she pull away from him.

The feel of her next to him, touching him, brought back so many memories. They used to walk along the beach at night just like this, listening to the surf wash up on the sand, watching the moonlight reflect on the water. They'd talked for hours about everything and nothing. Their most vivid childhood memories. Their favorite movies. Books. Even sports, though Ben always suspected she was humoring him, letting him ramble on about the New England Patriots. The six months they'd spent together had been the most satisfying of Ben's life. The happiest since his mother had died.

"Hey, I forgot. You're on vacation for your birthday. When is it?"

She wrinkled her nose. "It was yesterday."

He came to a halt and faced her. "Why didn't you tell

me? I could have—" He stopped. They'd spent the day anticipating the meeting at Mallory Square. Not exactly a relaxing time.

A grin stole across her face. "What? Thrown me a surprise party? I had enough surprises yesterday, thank you."

"Well, I could have at least told you happy birthday."

"Thank you." They continued walking, still close to each other, their steps matched. She watched her feet as they walked. "Ben, I want to talk to you about something." He sensed the tension in her body, in the set of her shoulders. "Something important."

Oh, no. She wants me to pray with her again.

Although, if the answers to Nikki's prayers always came as quickly as the last one, maybe he shouldn't be so quick to discount the practice.

Don't be ridiculous. It was a coincidence, nothing more, that the boat came at exactly that time.

"O-kay." He drew the word out. "I think I know what you want to say. But let me just—"

A sudden movement from the shadows behind a wooden structure startled him into silence. In the next instant, something hard pressed into the center of his back.

"*Hola,* amigo. We meet again."

High tenor. Heavily accented. It took a minute, but then he placed the voice. Key West. Mouth, from the pier at Mallory Square.

A second man emerged from the shadow and stepped in front of them. Inside the circle of Ben's arm, Nikki's body went rigid. The guy Ben had knocked into the water. He wore a dangerous scowl as he glared at Ben. Obviously, he was holding a major grudge.

"I see you enjoyed an afternoon dive. Hand over the thumb drive now and all is forgiven." Señor Mouth's voice in his ear rang with false geniality, even as the gun pressed into his back. "Of course, if you do not intend to keep your part of our bargain, I have permission to deal with you and the *señorita* however I want."

Beside Ben, Nikki sucked in a loud, shuddering breath.

THIRTEEN

They were pushed into the shadows behind the storage building where the men had been hiding. Nikki sought strength from Ben's arm around her waist and stayed close to him. When they were allowed to stop, the second man, the one who had grabbed her in Key West, stood directly in front of her and watched her with an unwavering stare as black as the shark's a few hours before. She shrank even closer to Ben's side.

Ben gave a weak laugh. "You guys obviously need to work on your communication skills."

How could he speak so calmly with a gun barrel pressed against his back? The only thing keeping her teeth from chattering in terror was the fact that she had them clenched together. Her knees were locked, frozen. Had they not been, no doubt they wouldn't have held her upright. How much stress could a person take before she collapsed under the strain?

"My English is good. You understand me," replied the man with the gun.

"No, I mean communication within your own organization. Or maybe you're just too far down the totem pole to get up-to-the-minute scoop."

Ben laughed again, this time with a touch of derision.

Nikki shot him a warning glance. *Don't taunt him, Ben. He has a gun.*

"I gave the records to your buddies." Sarcasm weighed down his words. "You know, the nice ones who stole our boat and tried to turn us into supper for the sharks."

"Ah, you make a joke. I do not like jokes, *señor.* Just give us the item."

The danger in the man's voice sent a shiver rippling through Nikki's body. She spoke up before Ben could provoke him further.

"He's not joking. Some of your people were waiting when we surfaced with the flash drive. They took it and then baited the water for sharks before they left."

A pause. "Our people?"

"Four men." She shot a quick backward glance at the handgun pressed between Ben's shoulder blades. "They had bigger guns, though."

A heavy silence fell over their captors. The eyes of the man standing in front of them did not waver from his partner's face. As Nikki watched, an unspoken message passed between them. The man's forehead cleared. In the next instant, he lurched forward, grabbed Nikki's arm in an iron grip and jerked her away from Ben.

Fear paralyzed her lungs.

"Hey!" Ben's hand formed a fist and he started to lunge for the guy, but froze when the gun moved up his spine to the base of his skull.

"We go for a ride, yes?" The gun nudged Ben's head forward. Nikki choked on a sob. "Someplace where we can talk."

"There's nothing to say," Ben almost shouted. "Make a call. You'll find out we're telling the truth. We've already turned over the list."

The man holding Nikki pulled her to the corner of the building and shoved her against the rough wood while he peeked around. She gasped, more from fear than pain. A sobering fact became clear in that instant. The Reynosa cartel never intended to let them live. They wanted to get rid of anyone who knew about the information. When these two called whoever was in charge of getting the flash drive back, they would be instructed to kill them.

God, please don't let us die. But if we do, please watch over Joshua. The thought of her innocent baby in the hands of these murderers squeezed her heart in a painful vise. *Keep him safe from these horrible people.*

Her captor half pushed, half dragged her out of the shadows and toward a nearby parking lot. Ben was close behind. She couldn't see him, but heard the scuff of the gun-wielder's shoes on the walkway as they followed. They passed no one on the way to the parking lot, where only a few cars were scattered. When she stepped off the pavement, gravel bit into the bottom of her bare feet.

"Listen, when you make that phone call, you can give your boss a message for me." Though outwardly calm, Ben's clipped words betrayed a hint of strain. "Tell him if he kills us, he'll be making a mistake. I have a copy of that data. If I die, it'll be found, and there's some pretty powerful people who are going to have a lot to answer for."

Was he bluffing? Nikki couldn't see his face to be sure, but if so, it was a good bluff. And making a copy sounded like something Ben would do.

They were heading for a dirty white car parked at the far side of the lot. The skin on Nikki's arm burned beneath the rough fingers of her captor as he shoved her forward. What would happen to them once they were in that car? Would they be taken into the miles and miles of bush that covered the island and shot? If so, their bodies would never be found.

Oh, Joshua, you'll be an orphan.

She tried to walk lightly, but he forced her to move at an uncomfortable pace. A sharp rock sliced into her heel and sent a shaft of pain up her leg. Breath hissed through her teeth as tears stung in her eyes.

Behind her, wheels crunched on gravel. The man holding her glanced over his shoulder, and then jerked her to an abrupt halt.

Nikki turned. The sight that greeted her was the most beautiful thing she'd ever seen. A white car with a blue-and-red light bar across the top, and the words *Policía* in blue letters on the front fender.

Relief poured out of her in a grateful sob.

Thank You, God! Thank You.

Her captor's grip lessened. He didn't release her, but looped his hand casually through her arm, as though he was merely assisting her to the car. The other man swept the gun behind his back and stepped up beside Ben. From where she stood, Nikki saw the barrel still pointing in Ben's direction, the man's finger still on the trigger.

The window swept down, and the uniformed officer inside the car peered at them, suspicion heavy on his dark features. *"¿Está bien aquí?"*

Nikki held her body in a boardlike stiffness and tried to communicate her fear wordlessly, with her eyes. *Help us!*

The finger on the gun wavered as the Reynosa man answered. *"Estamos bien, gracias."*

"Actually, officer, we're glad you're here." Ben's words, loud after the quiet response of his captor, dripped with an exaggerated southern drawl. He grabbed Nikki's hand. "We're tourists, staying in a time-share up in Cancun, you know? We rode the ferryboat over to hang out for the day, and wouldn't you know it, we took a walk down the beach and got lost. Left our shoes, our clothes, everything, back there with our beach towels. Isn't that right, honey?"

Even in the midst of her fight to control the hysterical tears that threatened to burst forth any second, Nikki admired Ben's quick thinking. She squeezed his hand and nodded at the skeptical police officer.

Ben pulled her toward the car, out of their captors' reach. "These here fellas offered to give us a ride back to the beach. What was the name of that beach again, honey?"

The officer looked at her, waiting for an answer. Nikki's mind blanked for a moment, then she spouted the first beach she could remember. "Sunset Beach, wasn't it?"

Ben snapped his fingers. "That's right. We walked a long way, I can tell you that."

When he opened the patrol car's rear door, the police officer twisted around in the seat, eyebrows high.

"Anyway, we sure appreciate you showing up when you did, 'cause now these men won't have to be bothered with us. The people at our condo, they told us if we have *any* trouble at all, we should flag down a police officer, 'cause you guys are just great at helping tourists in trouble." He assisted her into the car and kept up a running monologue while she slid across the vinyl. Before he joined her, he grinned toward the silent Reynosa operatives. "Thanks for the offer, fellas. We sure appreciate how nice everybody here in Mexico has been."

He slid into the seat beside Nikki and slammed the door. She looked past him, though the window, where both Reynosa men stood watching with dumbfounded expressions, as though they couldn't understand how they'd just lost their captives.

The officer hesitated, his glance going from the two standing outside the car, to the rearview mirror and the two "tourists" in his backseat. Nikki held her breath. Would he buy Ben's story, or would he demand more answers? She closed her eyes.

Go. Please, just go. Before the guy with the gun decides to do something foolish.

The car rolled slowly forward. Breath whooshed out of her lungs. Beside her, Ben wilted against the seat back. The officer made a wide circle through the gravelly lot, then pulled onto the main street. Nikki twisted around to look through the rear window. The two Reynosa men broke from their astonished trance and ran across the parking lot toward the white car.

She exchanged a glance with Ben. They would try to catch up, though the traffic here on Cozumel's main road was heavy. Even if they didn't overtake the police car, the men would head for Sunset Beach and try to recapture them there. Or maybe they would just call their Reynosa boss and someone else would be waiting for them at Sunset Beach. Like the scary men from the boat this afternoon.

A wave of hopelessness washed over her. Where could they go? Not long ago they could have called Cesar for help. If the Reynosa cartel thought they'd been eaten by sharks, the watch on his home and dive shop would have been called off. But now they'd be watched even more closely than before. A call to Cesar would be certain danger for a kind man to whom they'd already brought nothing but trouble.

Another thought struck her, and the force nearly made her weep with terror. The Reynosa cartel had her passport. They knew her name. If they had powerful contacts within the United States, like Senator Webb, they'd be able to find out where she lived. Would they discover that she had a son?

Oh, God, please protect Joshua.

The officer's eyes became visible in the rearview mirror as he glanced toward them. "I don't like to tell you this, my friends, but if you left your belongings on the beach, they are gone."

Ben's shoulders heaved with an embarrassed laugh. "I was thinking the same thing a while ago. Pretty stupid of us, huh? Is there an American Consulate here?"

"*Sí,* but it will not open until tomorrow afternoon." The man shrugged. "We are a small island, and it is only an extension office. I suggest you call your resort in Cancun. Maybe they have another property here on Isla Cozumel where you can stay for the night. They can arrange to bring you back there tomorrow."

"Yeah. That's a good idea." Ben's lack of enthusiasm sounded in his voice.

The officer peered at them in the mirror again. "You have a cell phone? If not, you can use the phone at the police station."

Nikki stiffened in the seat. Wait a minute! She did know someone on Cozumel.

"No." The word came out louder than she intended. She flashed a quick smile toward the officer's reflection. "You've been very kind, and I hate to ask you to go out of your way, but could you take us somewhere else?"

There was one place in Cozumel where she had friends. Where she would feel safe. She flashed a quick glance at Ben before making her request.

"Could you take us to the church on Avenue 80?"

FOURTEEN

The church had hardly changed at all in the two-and-a-half years since Nikki's last visit. The cinder block had faded to a paler yellow, and the arched, wooden door needed to be sanded and repainted, but those were the only visible changes. A light shone through the vertical blinds in the single window of the small converted house, in what Nikki knew was the sanctuary. Strains of music drifted to them from inside, accompanying the sound of a female voice.

The police officer left them on the street in front of the church building. Ben stood, unmoving, and stared at the window. Salt had stiffened his curls into an unruly brown mop, and she fought the urge to brush them away from his forehead. His shoulders were stiff as rods, and he wore a look of absolute dread, as though he'd rather face Reynosa henchmen than a church service.

Nikki slipped a hand through his arm and pulled him toward the door. "Come on. They'll help us."

"They'll help *you.*" His feet did not move. "They hate me."

Astonished, Nikki stopped tugging on his arm. "What on earth would make you say that?"

"I know what they think of me. I'm the reprobate

who lured you into a life of sin." She almost wilted at the strength of his glare. "And they're the ones who rescued you from me."

She could hardly believe her ears. "Is that what you thought?"

"Well, what else was I supposed to think? Everything was going fine between us, and then you started coming here." He stabbed a finger toward the building. "Next thing I knew, you were talking about marriage and starting a family." He jerked around and turned his back toward the church. "My father was right about churches. He told me when I was ten years old that they're full of people who stick their noses in other people's business and accuse them of *sinning*." Ben glared at her. "Their plan sure worked with you. You stopped sinning. You left me."

Stunned, Nikki didn't know how to respond to this barrage of bitterness. When she had made the decision to leave Cozumel, she'd known Ben would be upset. But she thought he would be angry with her. She had no idea he'd blame the church.

I was wrong not to tell him.

The realization hit her with force. All this time, she thought she had done the right thing by leaving with no explanation. By saving him from giving up the life he loved.

"Ben, it wasn't like that. They never condemned you, or me, either. They just…loved me. More than that, they told me that Jesus loved me, no matter how much I'd messed up my life."

"See, that's what I mean." He almost spat the bitter words, as though he couldn't wait to get them out of his mouth. "I'm the one who messed up your life. You were responsible until you met me, a good girl who went to college and got a job and did everything right."

"Responsible, maybe, but I wasn't good." If only she could make him understand. She laid a hand on his arm. "When I started coming to the services here, I was so unhappy. I had some serious decisions to make, and I had nowhere to turn. Denise and Pastor Thomas didn't condemn me. They led me to realize how much I needed a Savior. But that need didn't start when I moved in with you. My need started the moment I was born."

Confusion drew deep creases between his eyes. "That's crazy."

"No, it's not." She was handling this badly. There were so many things she needed to tell him. About Jesus's love and how He had changed her life, given her hope. About Joshua. But now was not the time, nor the place. They had to get off the street. "Just come inside. They'll help us, I know they will."

She tugged, and this time he came with her. Slowly, dragging his feet across the broken sidewalk, he allowed her to lead him to the church.

At the door, Nikki paused and glanced down at her wrinkled T-shirt, her filthy bare feet. They both looked awful. Her fingers couldn't begin to tame the mangled mess of her hair.

She gave a nervous laugh. "This used to be a 'come as you are' church. I hope that hasn't changed."

"If you're having second thoughts—"

Ben started to back away, but she held tight to his arm. With the other hand, she opened the door and pulled him inside.

The small sanctuary had not changed. A faded banner on the mint green walls proclaimed *Jesús es el Señor*.

Three rows of white plastic chairs, not all of them occu-
pied, formed a half circle around the battered music
stand Pastor Thomas used to hold his notes when he
preached. Beside it stood a young Mexican woman,
strumming a guitar and singing. The worshipers sat
with their backs to the door, but when the singer caught
sight of them, she faltered and fell silent. A dozen heads
turned their way. Nikki scanned the astonished faces,
looking for a familiar one.

"Nikki!"

A woman on the front row hurried around the group
of chairs toward her, a tall man in shorts and sandals
close on her heels. A few more lines creased the face of
the American woman who rushed to her, and the few
strands of dark hair Nikki remembered joined the rest of
gray, but there was no mistaking her friend's identity.

"Denise! Oh, thank goodness."

Nikki released Ben and threw herself into Denise's
arms. The tears she'd fought so hard to hold back for the
past few hours poured down her cheeks. For a moment
all she could do was cling to her friend and let them
flow.

But there was no time for that.

She whispered, "Denise, we're in trouble. Bad trouble.
We need help."

No hesitation. No questions. Denise cast a silent
glance at her husband, Pastor Thomas, who turned
toward the curious onlookers.

"*Sigamos.*" The pastor waved his hands in circles in
the air. "Let's continue."

The singer strummed a chord on her guitar and picked
up the song again. Pastor Thomas returned to his seat in
the front row, while Denise guided Nikki out the front

door. She nodded for Ben to follow and he did. Rather meekly, Nikki thought.

When the door closed behind them, Denise headed toward the house next door, where she and Pastor Thomas lived. Nikki's knees wobbled, and her friend supported her with an arm around her waist.

"You poor thing, you're shivering. And you're not wearing any shoes. Do you have any fresh clothes?"

Nikki couldn't squeeze a word past the relieved tears that clogged her throat. She shook her head.

"Well, I'm sure we can find something in the donation box. It might not be stylish, but it'll be clean." She looked at Ben, who trailed behind them. "We haven't met. I'm Denise Evans. My husband Thomas and I serve at the church here."

Nikki heard Ben's mumbled response. "Ben Dearinger."

Denise's step faltered. She turned a loaded gaze on Nikki, her eyebrows arched high on her forehead. But her voice held nothing but welcome. "Nice to meet you, Ben. I'm sure we can find some clean clothes for you, too."

Denise pushed open the front door of the house and entered. She closed the door behind them.

"I'm dying to hear what's going on, but maybe it would be best if we wait until Thomas can join us. The service ends in another fifteen minutes, and I'm sure he'll hurry home." She folded her arms across her chest and swept a measuring glance over each of them. "In the meantime, let's find you two some clothes."

Nikki grabbed her hand. "Thank you, Denise. You're a godsend. But before I do anything, I have to make a phone call to the States. May I use your phone? I'll pay you back for the call, I promise."

She laughed. "Oh, sweetie, I call my daughter in Denver every Friday and talk to my grandchildren for an hour. One more call won't even be noticed on my phone bill."

Nikki and Ben trailed her through the small living room into the kitchen, where Denise retrieved her cell phone from the kitchen counter. She unplugged the cord that dangled from it and handed the phone to Nikki. "There you go. Fully charged."

Nikki clutched the phone in both hands. She glanced at Ben. Though he would hate being left alone with Denise, she couldn't make this call in front of him. The news that he had a son needed to be delivered with a little more finesse than overhearing a frantic phone call.

"Uh, would you two excuse me?" She gave an apologetic half shrug.

Ben looked startled, but Denise pushed her gently toward the hallway. "There's a chair in the spare bedroom. Ben and I will go out on the back porch and find you two some clothes and shoes."

Nikki didn't risk another look at Ben's face, but made a hasty escape, punching numbers on the phone as she went.

In the bedroom, she sank onto the chair in a corner as the line rang.

Please pick up. Please pick up.

"Hello?"

Relief whooshed out of her in a loud sigh. "Allison, thank goodness you're there. I'm in so much trouble, and I need your help."

"Don't tell me you got mugged again."

"No. I'm stranded in Mexico with no passport and some really, really bad people are trying to kill me."

Silence. "Nikki, if this is some kind of joke, it's not funny."

"It's no joke. I wish it were. It's a long story, and I don't have time to tell it in detail, but here's what happened."

She perched on the edge of the hard chair and sketched a quick summary of events since she had last talked to her friend. Only twenty-four hours before, but it seemed like weeks. About the contents of the thumb drive, she remained vague. No sense getting Allison any more involved than she had to be, for her own safety.

"And then Ben told them that he'd made a copy of the information, and if we died, it would surface and get a lot of important people in trouble. And right after he said that, a police officer pulled into the parking lot." She heaved a sigh as she wrapped up the account. "We got away, but I know they're looking for us."

"Wow. I'm stunned. I hardly know what to say."

Nikki closed her eyes and rubbed. They burned, from salt and exhaustion and too many pent-up tears. "I know it's hard to believe, but I promise it's true."

"You know what I find hardest believe? You reconnected with Joshua's father and didn't tell me."

Nikki ignored the tiny hint of accusation in her friend's voice. One thing she'd learned about her friend in the months since they became close, Allison loved to know intimate details. "I was going to tell you all about it when I got back. He was sitting right beside me when we talked last night. So I wasn't really free to dish any details. And I did have a few other pressing matters on my mind."

"Sounds like it." She whistled softly. "So do you think he really does have a copy of that record? 'Cause maybe you could use it as, like, a bargaining chip or something."

"Knowing Ben, he probably does. But listen, Allison. I need a huge favor from you."

"Anything. You want me to wire you money? I'll empty my bank account. I can lay my hands on a couple thousand as soon as the bank opens in the morning, and I'll scrape up more if you need it."

"No, nothing like that." She hesitated. "At least, not yet. What I really need is for you to take care of my mom and Joshua. Maybe even let them come stay at your place for a few days, just in case these people try to…to…" She couldn't finish the thought. It was too horrible to say.

She didn't need to. Allison understood.

"Absolutely. I'll go over there as soon as we hang up. Uh, are you going to call her and tell her what's going on?"

"I don't know." She scrubbed at her forehead, trying to force her brain to think clearly. "Mom tends to freak out, so I don't want to upset her. But she needs to know how serious the situation is so she'll take extra precautions."

The phone line was silent for a moment. When Allison spoke again, her voice was hesitant. "Listen, I don't want to sound overly paranoid or anything, but if these people are as powerful as you say they are, and if they really wanted to find out who you were, they probably knew before they got your passport. I mean, the time-share resort office has your name and address, right?"

Nikki wilted slowly against the chair as she considered the ramifications of Allison's words. "That means they might already know were my mother lives."

"Hey, I'm sure they're fine. I called her this afternoon to check on them, like you asked me to do last night. They were just coming home from church. But if these people do know where she lives, would they be able to tap her phone? If you tell her what's going on, they'll hear."

Nikki covered her face with her free hand. "You're right. What should I do?"

She could almost hear her friend's thoughts whirling on the other side of the phone. Her own brain felt fried. She couldn't come up with a single idea.

"Okay, how about this. What if you call her now, after we hang up, and act normal? Like nothing's wrong. Tell her we've talked, and I'm going to be dropping by to check on them. You know, give her a hand with Joshua. That way she'll be expecting me. I can explain everything in person, and I'll convince her to come to my apartment for a few days."

Nikki grasped at the suggestion like a lifesaver thrown to a drowning victim. "That's a great idea."

"I just hope whatever phone you're using isn't being tapped too. Where are you anyway?"

Nikki glanced around the bedroom. "With friends. They run a small church down here. I don't think anyone will look for us here."

A humorless laugh. "Yeah, they don't sound like the kind of people who go to church." She paused. "Oh, I'd better clean my apartment. I wasn't expecting anybody's mother to come over."

"Don't worry about it," Nikki told her. "Mom will probably clean it for you."

"Hey, there's the silver lining!"

Nikki managed a weak smile. "Allison, how can I ever thank you for doing this?"

"Just stay safe. Call me tomorrow when you talk to the American Consulate. Then we'll figure out what to do after you're safely back on American soil."

Safely back. With powerful people like Senator Webb in cahoots with Mexican organized crime, she wasn't sure she'd ever feel safe in her own country again. "I'll call the minute we know what we're doing."

Nikki hung up the phone and bowed her head over it. She'd had more scares in the past few hours than most people had in a lifetime, and the stress was taking its toll. Exhaustion was catching up with her. She could barely engage a coherent thought.

She drew in a deep breath and forced her eyes open. One more phone call, and she needed to sound normal. She glanced at her watch. Almost eight o'clock, which meant almost six in Portland. Joshua would just be having supper.

Leaning back in the chair, she punched in her mom's phone number.

FIFTEEN

Ben pulled the comb Denise said he could use through his towel-dried hair and inspected his reflection in the mirror on the back of the bathroom door. The shorts and T-shirt he'd selected from a well-stocked shelf on the enclosed porch were faded, but at least they fit. And clean clothes felt terrific. He unbuttoned the pocket on his swim trunks and transferred his camera to one of the deep pockets in his new-used shorts.

Denise kinda reminded him of his mother back when he was a kid, before cancer transformed her into a wraith. And he had to admit, Denise seemed nice for a church lady. Genuinely nice, not fake nice like most of the goody-goody people he'd known. She hadn't tried to preach at him, yet. He'd figured she would whip out her Bible and start thumping on it the minute Nikki left the room.

What was Nikki up to, anyway? She'd still been on the phone when he got in the shower, her voice nothing but an indistinguishable drone through the walls.

Probably calling her boyfriend back home.

Did she have a boyfriend? The idea filled him with gloom. The question had pressed on him ever since he first caught sight of her on the dock in Key West. He was afraid to ask, though. There for a few seconds, back in the water, and again on the dock at the marina, Ben thought she was warming up to him again. She had responded when he kissed her. For a moment, he almost hoped—

Cut it out. I'm nothing but a paragraph in her diary. Someone she won't tell her kids about when she's married and settled and this nightmare is behind her.

Of course, they had a lot of ground to cover before either of them could get back home.

And where was home? For Nikki it was Oregon, where she grew up and where her mother lived. But what about him? He hadn't had a place he truly thought of as home in years, not since his mother died. There was nothing for him in Phoenix, where he had lived when he was a boy. His current residence was in the Florida Keys, but that wasn't home. Key West and, before that, Cozumel were merely the most recent in a whole list of temporary locations he'd drifted to in his search of... what? The carefree lifestyle his father had enjoyed? Since Nikki's departure over two years ago, a realization had been growing inside him. That lifestyle wasn't all it was cracked up to be. Sure, it sounded terrific having no responsibilities, no ties. But did he really want to live like this forever?

Ben folded his damp towel and draped it over the edge of the tub. When this was all over, he had some decisions to make. But that was in the future. The way things were looking now, he might not even live that long. He gathered his dirty clothes and headed for the kitchen.

A delicious aroma struck him when he entered the room and stirred up a rumble in his empty stomach.

A wave of weakness threatened to knock him off his feet. When had they eaten last? A bag of potato chips, grabbed from a gas station in Mérida on their way out of town. So much had happened since then, that seemed like days ago.

Nikki jumped up from a chair at the small table and picked up the clothes Denise had selected for her. "My turn." She smiled as she approached the doorway. "You look much better."

He started to quip a response, something about how a shower would improve her looks too, but the words died on his tongue. They wouldn't be true. Even dirty and disheveled, with her hair dried in chunky dreadlocks, she was stunning.

Instead, he said the first thing that came to mind. "Everything okay at home?" The words came out bitter.

Her eyebrows arched, but then she seemed embarrassed and mumbled as she edged around him, "Everything's fine."

When the bathroom door closed behind her, Ben turned to find two sets of eyes watching him. Denise stood at the counter, and the tall man he'd seen over at the church sat at the table. He stood and crossed the small room in two long-legged steps.

"Hello, Ben. I'm Thomas Evans." He shook Ben's hand with a firm grip.

"Nice to meet you, sir." Ben glanced at Denise and hefted his dirty clothes. "I figure I might as well donate these. You know, kind of a trade."

"Thank you, Ben. Just toss them out on the back porch in that box by the door."

He did as instructed and joined Thomas at the table.

Denise placed a full glass of orange juice in front of him.

"Drink this. You need some calories in your system. I'm heating up some *chile rellenos* a woman in our congregation makes. I keep a few in the freezer for quick meals."

Ben inhaled. "It does smell good, ma'am." He picked up the glass and gulped half the juice.

Thomas waited until Ben set the glass down to speak. "While you were in the shower, Nikki filled us in on your situation." He shook his head. "I wish I could say I was shocked, but organized crime is prevalent here in Mexico. Frankly, I think it's a miracle you're alive."

The emphasis he gave *miracle* made it more than a figure of speech. Until a few hours ago, Ben would have scoffed at the idea that miracles existed. But the sight of that fishing boat, coming within a few seconds after he and Nikki said Amen... Well, the timing was nothing short of amazing.

"I guess Nikki told you about our, uh, rescue."

Thomas nodded. His hair, more silver than brown, formed an *M* at his hairline and his scalp showed through on top. "She's convinced the arrival of that fishing boat was an answer to prayer. I tend to agree with her. I've seen God go to some pretty extreme measures to answer the prayers of His children."

Ben picked up his glass. "I don't know. He sure hasn't answered any of mine."

The man leaned forward, his eyes kind. "How often have you asked, son?"

Here it comes. A sermon, and with Nikki in the shower, I'm stuck here for the full brunt of it.

Thomas didn't wait for his answer. "Some people

have a hard time believing in a loving Father who takes an active role in the lives of His children. Not me. I've seen a lot of things during my years here in Mexico. I know God comes through for His kids."

"Thomas, don't pester the boy." Denise scolded her husband as she pulled a bowl out of a microwave and set another in its place. "He's been through a lot in the past few days."

Her husband sent an apologetic smile across the table toward Ben. "Sorry. She's right. I tend to get carried away when I talk about my heavenly Dad, you know?"

"Your heavenly Dad?" Ben laughed and traced a circle in the condensation on the cool glass. "I've never heard anyone refer to God like that."

Thomas shrugged. "That's who He is to me. He's proved it over and over."

The idea of a dad who actually came through for his kids, who took care of them, was beyond Ben's experience. Dads were fun, but they weren't reliable. They couldn't be counted on. At least, not Ben's.

What if these people are right? What if God really does love and protect His kids? What if He really does care?

Yet another thing Ben would have to have to devote some time to thinking about later, when this ordeal was over.

"Denise is right, though." Thomas straightened in his chair. "What we need to focus on now is how to get you two back home safely. What are your plans, and how can we help?"

"Wel-l-l." Ben drew the word out while he tried to think. "I guess we'll go to the American Consulate office when it opens tomorrow and report our passports as stolen. And hope they can help get us home. After that…" Ben hesitated. Could he trust these people? He glanced from Thomas to Denise, busy stirring the steaming contents of a bowl, and decided he could. "Did Nikki tell you about the list?"

Thomas nodded. "She didn't tell us what it contained, though."

"It's probably best if you don't know. When we get back to the States, I'm going to put Nikki on a plane back home, where she'll be safe. Then I'm going to call someone. I don't know who. The FBI, maybe, or Homeland Security. That information implicated some high-up muckety-mucks. I don't know who I can trust."

The older man leaned forward and reached across the table to place a hand over Ben's. "I'm going to pray you know exactly what to do."

Though he never would have dreamed it possible, the idea of Thomas praying for him gave Ben a flicker of hope that maybe this nightmare would turn out okay after all.

Nikki entered the room, her clean, wet hair combed straight back from her forehead. Ben's breath caught in his throat at the sight of her.

What did somebody like her ever see in me to begin with? No wonder she left me.

Their last argument returned to him with force, every word of it. She'd been attending church—this church, with Denise and Thomas—for a few weeks, and suddenly she'd started hinting about "making things legal." Ben had sensed the steel jaws of matrimony about to snap closed on him, and he had panicked. Told her that he would never settle down, never give up his carefree life. And at the time, he meant it, every word of it.

But looking at her now, with her face clean and glowing from the heat of her shower, doubts washed over him. What kind of jerk was he? Who let a woman like Nikki get away?

"They're a little big." Nikki tugged at the waistband of the donated shorts. "But they'll be fine."

Denise turned from the counter with a bowl in her hands and eyed her. "I think there are some smaller ones out there you can try. But first, sit down and eat something."

She set a bowl of black beans on the table in front of Ben, then rice, and finally, a plate of *chile rellenos*. "I wish I had something better to feed you. These are just some leftovers I threw together."

Ben inhaled the fragrant steam wafting from the beans. An answering rumble of anticipation vibrated in his stomach. "Are you kidding? This is awesome. Thank you."

Nikki slid into the chair beside him. "Pastor Thomas, would you bless the food?"

"Certainly."

The three of them bowed their heads. Ben hesitated only a second, and then did the same.

SIXTEEN

Nikki awoke with a start. Dark room. Stifling heat. Where was she? She sat up in the narrow bed. Her mind floundered in the dark while her eyes struggled to make out details by the dim light seeping through an open window.

Then she remembered. Ben. The flash drive. Denise and Pastor Thomas. And the Reynosa cartel.

She collapsed on the pillow and willed her heartbeat to return to normal. Wispy memories of the dream that awakened her floated through her mind, of blue-tinted water and bubbles and sharks. She willed them to go, to leave her mind clear and empty so she could go back to sleep. Above her, a paddle fan whirled and tried to cool her by bathing her body in warm, stale air. She opened her eyes and glanced at the window. The curtains hung limp, without a breeze to give them life. She'd modestly closed the door when she went to bed, but without the benefit of a cross breeze, she'd confined herself to an oven.

What was Joshua doing right now? Had Allison made a bed for him on the floor in her room, or was he in the living room, with Mom asleep on Allison's comfy sofa? Or maybe Allison generously gave up her bedroom for

Mom and Joshua. Wherever they slept, no doubt they were all snuggled beneath blankets, warm inside while the chilly Oregon wind blew at the windows.

I could sure use a little of that wintery cold right now.

Impossible to sleep in this heat. Maybe a drink of water would cool her off. She heaved herself out of bed and slipped her donated shorts on beneath the oversized nightshirt Denise had given her.

She opened the door slowly, in case it creaked and woke everyone in the small house, and tiptoed out into the hallway. A snore came from the other bedroom, where Pastor Thomas and Denise slept. From the direction of the living room came the sound of Ben's deep, even breathing. Moving as silently as she could, she crept into the kitchen. Moonlight filtered through a window to fill the comfy room with a white glow. Nikki took a glass from the cabinet and filled it with water from a pitcher in the refrigerator.

Ah. Cold and wet. Exactly what she needed.

Except now she was wide awake. What time was it, anyway? The clock on the wall read almost one. She'd fallen asleep around eight-thirty, shortly after the dinner Denise served them, unable to stave off exhaustion another minute.

One o'clock here would only be eleven o'clock back home. Joshua would have long since fallen asleep, but Allison and Mom might still be awake. Denise's phone lay on the counter. Would she mind one more international call? No, a generous person like Denise wouldn't mind a dozen calls. Besides, Nikki fully intended to reimburse her for the calls, no matter how she protested.

And it would help Nikki to sleep, hearing Allison's voice, knowing Joshua and Mom were safe in her care.

Nikki picked up the phone and crept out the back door and through the screened porch, where she sat on the small stoop. The moon shone brightly in the sky and illuminated the tiny backyard. She pressed in Allison's number and held the phone to her ear.

No answer. On the fifth ring, she hung up before voice mail could kick in.

An uneasy feeling pressed at the edges of her mind. Why wouldn't Allison answer the phone? Even if she had gone to bed, she'd hear the phone ring, wouldn't she? She wouldn't ignore the call, in case Nikki phoned again. With quick fingers, Nikki tried the call a second time.

Again, no answer.

Now fully worried, she attempted to calm her racing thoughts. What if something had happened to them? A number of possibilities came to mind, but only one flashed like a lighthouse in the midst of the storm raging in her head—the Reynosa people had found them.

Calm down. Don't jump to conclusions. Maybe her phone is in the car or something. There are a million reasons she might not answer a call.

With shaking fingers, Nikki dialed her mother's number. There would probably be no answer, because Mom would have left with Allison hours ago, but she had to—

The phone was answered before the first ring completed. "Hello? Allison, is that you?"

Dread dropped like a stone into Nikki's stomach. "No, Mom, it's me."

"Oh, Nikki, I'm so glad to hear your voice. I've been trying to call your cell phone for hours."

"What's wrong? Is Joshua okay?"

"I don't know." A sob broke the last word. "Your friend Allison dropped by, and she took him to get a kid's meal and play in the Playland. But they should have been back long before now."

Nikki's mind grasped at the words. "Allison took Joshua alone? She was supposed to take both of you."

"What? Why would she do that? She was giving me a break. When you called earlier you said she was going to come over and help me, and that's what she did."

"But Mom, didn't she explain everything? Didn't she offer to take you and Joshua to her apartment for a few days, until I can get home from Mexico?"

"Mexico? Nikki, what are you talking about? I thought you were in Florida."

Panic, full-blown and intense, exploded in her brain. Her breath came in hard, painful gasps.

Allison had lied to her.

But why? Had someone from the Reynosa cartel gotten to her? Did they threaten her if she didn't help them kidnap Joshua? Or—

A powerful nausea gripped her stomach, and she bent over double, retching.

Or did Allison work for Senator Webb?

It all made sense now. Allison taking the job at the finance company four months ago and working *so hard* to become her friend. Her oh-so-generous offer to use the time-share in Key West, which put Nikki on the same small island with Ben. Did her father own the time-share at all, or was the whole trip arranged just to get Nikki down there? And then, the gift certificate from Key West Water Adventures, was that part of the ruse?

"Mom." She gulped a shuddering breath. "That birthday present you sent me, the gift certificate. Whose idea was that?"

"What? What difference does that—"

"Mom! It's important. Whose idea was it?"

Nikki's hand trembled so badly she almost dropped the phone. She pressed it to her ear to steady it.

"Well." A pause. "It was Allison's. After you booked your flight, she called me and asked if I was planning to get you something special for your birthday. I told her I'd thought about a nice outfit, but she suggested a gift certificate for an excursion on your vacation."

A wail began from somewhere, and grew louder in Nikki's ears. It took her a minute to realize the sound was coming from her.

"Nikki, what's wrong? What's happening?"

She clamped her mouth shut. *Don't panic. You are no help to Joshua if you panic. Think!*

"Okay, listen to me, Mom. As soon as we hang up, call the police. Tell them what's happened. Tell them Joshua has been—" She drew in a shuddering breath. "Tell them Joshua has been kidnapped."

"Kidnapped? Oh, Nikki, no."

"Do it, Mom. Right now. I'll call you back when the police are there and explain everything to them."

As she punched the button to end the call, she leaped to her feet and jerked the back door open, screaming to wake everyone inside.

"They've got Joshua!"

She crossed the kitchen at a run and dashed into the living room. On the sofa, Ben was still sound asleep.

Nikki threw herself at him, shaking him by the shoulders. "Ben, Ben, wake up. They've got Joshua."

"Huh?" His eyes fluttered open, dull with sleep. "Who has Joshua? Who's Joshua?"

Denise and Pastor Thomas appeared from the bedroom, groggy and in their nightclothes. Someone flipped a switch, and light flooded the room.

"Joshua is my son." Nikki choked the words through a throat that burned with terror. "Ben, Joshua is *your* son. And they've kidnapped him."

She surrendered to the hysterical weeping she could no longer contain.

SEVENTEEN

The words didn't make sense. Ben sat up on the couch, a sobbing Nikki on her knees beside him. He squeezed his eyes shut and let the revelation marinate in his sleep-fogged brain.

Nikki has a son—and he's my *son.*

I have a son.

So that's why Nikki left Cozumel so suddenly. She'd discovered she was pregnant and was afraid to tell him. All those hints about settling down, about moving back to the States and getting a real job. She'd been feeling him out, trying to see how he'd react to the responsibility of having a family.

And he'd responded by shutting her down.

Denise hurried around the couch and stooped to place her arms around Nikki's heaving shoulders. "Shhh, calm down. You won't help anyone by being hysterical."

Amazing. The woman didn't seem at all surprised by Nikki's news. It was almost as if—

Ben jerked around on the cushion and speared Thomas with a glare. "You knew about this. About the baby."

The older man inclined his head. He didn't raise his

gaze to meet Ben's. "Nikki told us that she was pregnant the second or third time she attended services here."

Ben leaped off the couch. "You're the reason she left me, aren't you? You told her to get away from a loser like me, to go home and find somebody responsible." His hands clenched into fists, and he locked his elbows at his side so he wouldn't fly at the man and pummel him. "Admit it."

Thomas shook his head, his expression unruffled. "That's not true."

Nikki launched herself at Ben. She grabbed the front of his shirt in both fists and shook him. "That doesn't matter now. Don't you understand? Joshua is gone, kidnapped. *We've got to do something.*" She released him and ran into the kitchen. An instant later she returned with a cell phone and slammed it into Ben's chest. "Call the FBI or somebody. Tell them about the information about Senator Webb." Her voice broke. "Tell them they have to get my son back."

Her face crumpled, and loud sobs bent her double.

"Nikki, you need to calm down." Denise enfolded her in a strong embrace and pulled her toward the kitchen. "Come in here. We're going to pray, and then you're doing to drink some iced tea and wash your face. And then we'll figure out what to do."

As she spoke, the woman guided Nikki toward the kitchen. Before they left the room, she caught first her husband, then Ben, in a stern glare that said, in no uncertain terms, *You two make a plan while I calm her down.*

The minute they were out of the room, Thomas moved toward Ben. "Listen, son, when Nikki came here two-and-a-half years ago, she was confused and frightened.

We offered spiritual counsel, that's all. We never advised her about what action she should take."

Ben searched his face for telltale signs that the man was lying. Thomas met his gaze without flinching.

He's telling the truth.

"I'm sorry. It's just…" Ben covered his face with his hands and scrubbed, a feeble attempt to wipe away the confusion. "It's a shock, you know?"

Thomas laid a heavy hand on his shoulder. "I'm sure it is. Unfortunately, you don't have time to get used to the idea that you're a father. We need to do something, and quickly."

A father. Wow.

"Yeah." Ben straightened and jerked a nod. "Okay. A plan. First, we need to find out—"

A knock on the door interrupted him.

Ben exchanged a startled glance with Thomas, and they both whirled around. His watch read just after one o'clock in the morning. Whoever was on the other side of that door wasn't dropping by for a friendly visit.

"Do you have a gun?" Ben whispered.

"I'm a *pastor*." Thomas's reply came out as a hiss. "I don't have any reason to own a gun."

"Yeah? Well, the fact that there are probably murdering drug dealers on the other side of that door seems like a pretty good reason to me."

"Hold on." He dashed out of the room and returned in a second carrying a baseball bat, which he shoved at Ben. "Here. You stand behind the door. I'll answer it, and if they have a gun, hit them from behind."

Ben couldn't hold back a nervous chuckle. "That doesn't sound very pastorly, Pastor."

Thomas's mouth formed a grim line. "I'll offer to pray for them after we've disarmed them."

The knock came a second time, this one louder and more insistent. Nikki and Denise appeared in the doorway behind them, and Ben waved them back as he took up his position, the bat poised above his head. They retreated into the kitchen, out of sight.

Thomas placed a hand on the knob and inhaled a slow breath. He glanced at Ben, who nodded that he was ready, then swung the door open.

"May I help you?"

From his vantage point, Ben couldn't see who stood on the front stoop. But he was surprised when a polite male voice responded.

"We're sorry to disturb you, sir. We're looking for Benjamin Dearinger and Nicole Hoffman, and we have reason to believe they're here."

The heavy accent in the stranger's voice was not Spanish, but a slow Texas drawl. Ben lowered the baseball bat a fraction.

"I'm not sure—" Thomas began.

The man interrupted. "Sir, it's important that we speak with Ms. Hoffman and Mr. Dearinger. We have a message for them from Senator Adam Webb."

Nikki charged into the room, Denise close on her heels. Ben stepped around the open door, his free hand outstretched, but before he could stop her, she flew at the man on the front stoop. Her fists pummeled his chest in sync with her words.

"Where is Joshua? Give me back my son!"

EIGHTEEN

Someone came up behind Nikki, grabbed her arms and pulled her away from the startled man in the doorway. She fought against the constraint, until Ben's words seeped through her hysterical crying.

"Nikki, calm down. We'll find him. I promise. I'll do whatever I have to do, but we'll get him back."

She twisted around and collapsed against his chest. Strong arms encircled her, held her close.

"Oh, Ben." She buried her face in the soft skin of his neck. "Ben, he's only two. What if they don't feed him? What if they hurt him? What if—"

"Shhh. Don't think like that."

The embrace tightened, and then he gently pried her arms from around his neck. He faced the two men on the front stoop. Nikki clutched his strong arm with both hands and tried to get her heaving sobs under control.

"I've already turned over the flash drive to the Reynosa people." Ben's voice vibrated through her body. "So you can tell the senator there's no need to hold the boy. He's got what he wanted."

The men exchanged a glance. "You gave the records to someone from the Reynosa organization?" asked the first one.

She drew herself up, indignant. "Well, it's not like we had much of a choice. Did the senator tell them to feed us to the sharks, or did they do that on their own?"

Deep, confused lines appeared in both foreheads. "Ma'am?"

White-hot anger erupted, clearing away the last of Nikki's panic and leaving her clearheaded. She stepped away from Ben, and didn't bother to hide the full force of her fury as she faced the two messengers. "Don't tell me the senator didn't know what was going on. When he made a deal with murderers, he became a murderer himself. He's got a whole list of crimes he's going to have to answer for someday." She took a step forward, glaring. "And if he harms one hair on my baby's head..."

She let the threat go unnamed, mostly because she wasn't sure what she'd do. But one thing she did know—it would be terrible.

The men exchanged another glance, and then the first one said, "Excuse us for one moment, please."

As they stepped off the stoop, the second man unsnapped a leather cell phone case at his belt. They huddled together on the sidewalk, their backs to the house.

Ben pulled her into the room. "Uh, Nikki? That might not be the best way to convince them to return our son."

His words acted like ice water on the flames of her anger. He was right, of course. What was she doing, threatening someone as powerful as Senator Webb? And while he had Joshua, too?

She covered her face with her hands. "Oh, Ben. What are we going to do?"

He wrapped her in a hug. "Whatever we have to."

Pastor Thomas and Denise, who had been standing back while Nikki and Ben confronted the crooked senator's messengers, rounded the sofa and came to stand beside them.

"Right now, we're going to use the most powerful weapon at our disposal," Denise said. "We're going to pray."

Pastor Thomas looked at Ben. "All right with you, son?"

To Nikki's surprise, Ben nodded without a moment's hesitation. "Please do, sir."

The older couple wrapped their arms around them both. The four of them stood in a tight circle, heads bowed, while Pastor Thomas prayed.

"Lord, the situation looks hopeless right now, but You are the Giver of hope. Guide Nikki and Ben, and let them know the right path to take. We place Joshua in Your care, and we ask You to protect him. Keep constant watch over him, and return him to his parents safely. In Jesus's name we pray. Amen."

"Amen," Nikki and Ben echoed in unison.

She managed a trembling smile around the circle. "Thank you."

Footsteps scuffed on the concrete porch behind her. She turned to see the two men had returned to the doorway.

The first cleared his voice. "We need you to come with us."

Ben pushed her behind him and stood erect, his back stiff. "Nikki's not going anywhere. I'll go. I'm the one who got involved in this mess to begin with."

The second man shook his head. "I'm sorry, sir, but we'll need both of you to come."

Ben's body seemed to swell as he drew breath to protest, but Nikki stepped up beside him. It didn't matter one bit how this situation began. They were both involved now. "Where are we going?"

The first man responded. "To Texas. Senator Webb would like to meet with you."

While Nikki and Denise went into the other room to retrieve Nikki's shoes, Ben stood with Thomas in the living room. The senator's goons waited in a car out front.

"Listen, son, I want you to take this."

Thomas pressed something into Ben's hand. He looked down at a thin, folded stack of U.S. dollars. The one on top was a fifty.

He tried to hand it back. "Sir, I can't take this."

Thomas shoved his hands behind him. "Yes, you can, and you're going to. You don't know where you're going to end up after this meeting." His lips formed a grim line. "It's not much, only three hundred. We keep some American money stashed in a safe place, just in case."

Ben shook his head. "Really, I can't take your money."

Thomas caught his gaze and held it. "You're not on your own anymore, Ben. If—" He bit off the word, and corrected himself. "*When* you get the boy back, you might need this for food or shelter."

The words struck Ben with force. He wasn't on his own anymore. He had responsibilities. Other people depended on him. The realization squeezed in on him like a slowly tightening straitjacket.

With an effort, he filled his lungs. He'd deal with that later. First, they had to get Joshua back safely.

He slid the cash into his pocket and stuck his hand toward Thomas. "I'll pay you back as soon as I can."

The pastor caught his hand in a firm grip, then pulled him forward into a quick embrace. "I know you will."

He slapped him on the back and released him as Nikki and Denise returned.

"I'm ready."

The smile Nikki turned on him trembled a little, but at least she wasn't hysterical anymore. They would need all their wits about them if they were going to get their son back alive.

Our son. I'm a father.

Numb amazement still accompanied the thought.

Denise caught him in a farewell hug and whispered in his ear. "We'll be praying for you constantly."

"Thank you, ma'am. I can't tell you how much that means to me."

As he said the words, Ben realized how true they were. If God really was a powerful Father, a—what did Thomas call him? A heavenly Dad—then Ben and Nikki could sure use his help.

Did You hear that? He directed his thoughts outward. *We really could use some help getting Joshua back safely.*

There. He'd prayed. Sort of.

Nikki stepped away from Denise's farewell hug and turned a brave smile his way. "I'm ready."

Ben wasn't sure either of them was really ready for the meeting that lay ahead. The waters they were about to dive into were deeper than anything he'd ever attempted before. But he matched Nikki's smile and put an arm around her shoulders.

"Let's go."

NINETEEN

The five-and-a-half-hour flight passed in almost total silence. Sleep was impossible. Nikki tried to remain calm, but she couldn't stop thinking about how frightened Joshua must be. Surely Allison wouldn't hurt a child, would she? Her heart twisted in her chest as she tried to imagine what her baby was going through.

Hold on, Joshua. Mommy's coming.

She clutched Ben's hand across the aisle of the eight-passenger cabin, stared out the dark window and tried not to think about the terrible things that could happen to a scuba diver who flew within twenty-four hours of a dive.

Lord, please don't let us get an air embolism or the bends or anything like that.

She leaned sideways and whispered, "Are you worried about decompression sickness?"

Ben squeezed her hand and shook his head. "I think we would have felt the effects by now. Besides, did we have an option?" He cast a backward glance toward the senator's henchmen.

After driving Nikki and Ben to a private jet waiting at Cozumel's tiny airport, the senator's messengers had strapped themselves into the two rear seats and proceeded to assume a taciturn silence. At first Nikki and Ben sat in seats facing them, but when it became apparent that Nikki's questions and Ben's goading would not elicit a response, they moved up into the other pair of forward-facing seats, each lost in their own thoughts. Nikki realized Ben was right. If complying with Senator Webb's demand for a meeting would help her get Joshua back, then she would have done it regardless of the risk. A constant, silent prayer flew from her tortured soul toward heaven. After a while she ran out of words, and could only form a single plea: *please help us.*

The wheels touching down on the runway jolted her out of a semisleep. She looked out the window. Dark still, but the sun had just begun to lighten the eastern sky. An unbroken line of mountains stood in jagged silhouette beyond a sprawling city. A glance through the window on Ben's side showed more dark peaks. They'd just landed in a wide, flat valley between two mountain ranges. It didn't look like Texas to her.

"Where are we?" she asked Ben.

One of the men behind them broke his hours-long silence. "Salt Lake City."

Nikki and Ben exchanged a glance.

"I thought we were going to Texas," she said.

"Change of plans." No explanation, just that abrupt answer.

Why? She wanted to scream at them, but one backward look at their stony faces told her it would do no good. Tendrils of panic reached for her, tried to draw her emotions back into a frenzy, but she gritted her teeth and pushed them away. She had to stay clearheaded for Joshua.

The jet reached the end of the runway, turned and

taxied back in the direction they came. Snow, piled in tall mounds, lined the runway. Off to one side stood a small building, much smaller than she expected.

Ben ducked his head and looked through the window on her side of the plane. "We must be at a private airstrip. This place isn't nearly big enough to be Salt Lake's main airport."

Nikki glanced backward for verification, and one of the men nodded.

As the jet approached the building, Nikki caught sight of another small aircraft parked on the tarmac. Not far from it, a limousine awaited.

She faced Ben and twisted her lips. "I think our ride's here."

The jet rolled to a stop next to the other one. The engines had not powered down all the way before one of the silent men left his seat, opened the door and dropped a narrow set of stairs to the ground. Nikki and Ben navigated the stairs before the second man could get his seat belt unbuckled. Nikki's breath formed visible puffs in front of her face, and she shivered in the frigid cold. Their donated Mexican clothing was totally inappropriate for a chilly morning in Utah. Beside her, Ben folded his bare arms and rubbed his hands along them.

The door to the limousine opened. A man in a dark suit and blindingly white shirt emerged. He strode toward them, his expression inscrutable.

"Mr. Dearinger. Ms. Hoffman." He dipped his head to each of them as he addressed them. "My name is Paul Bentley. I'm Senator Webb's aide. I trust your flight was satisfactory."

Nikki wanted to fly at him, to slap the indifference off his face and demand to see her son. Ben must have sensed her reaction, because he stepped close to her, as though ready to hold her back if she tried.

"It was extremely uninformative," he replied, his voice heavy with sarcasm. "I hope those two goons back there don't ever try to get jobs as tour guides. They'd be lousy at it."

How he sounded so calm, Nikki couldn't imagine. When she looked at him, his eye twitched closed in a private wink that lessened the tense nerves knotting her insides.

He's right. We won't get anywhere with these people by making demands.

Mr. Stone Face didn't blink. "If you'll please come with me, the senator is waiting for you." He gestured toward the limo.

Nikki conquered her first instinct, which was to run to the car, fling open the door and jerk the senator out by the scruff of his neck. She forced herself to match Ben's sedate pace. The windows had been tinted black, rendering the interior invisible. When they arrived, the impeccably dressed man opened the door and gestured for them to enter. Nikki ducked inside first.

A dim, yellow glow lit the interior. Warmth engulfed her even as soft brown leather caressed her bare legs when she slid across to make room for Ben. She sank into the plush seat and looked around with wide eyes.

Crystal gleamed from a bar to her right, a flat-screen monitor embedded in the panel above it. Luxurious, high-backed bench seats curved in two semi circles facing each other. In the center space, folded sections of a newspaper lay atop a highly polished cherry tabletop. And across from her, one leg resting casually across the other as though he conducted meetings like this every day of his life, a familiar face studied her through slightly narrowed eyelids.

Senator Adam Webb.

Unlike Mr. Bentley, the senator was dressed casually in tan slacks. A cream-colored turtleneck protruded from the collar of a striped wool sweater. He uncrossed his legs and reached for a carafe on the bar. When he poured the dark steaming liquid into a china cup, the pungent odor of coffee flooded the limo. He picked up the cup, extended it toward her and asked, "Do you take cream and sugar, my dear?"

Numb, Nikki shook her head. He set the cup on the table between them and gently scooted it across the surface to her side.

When Ben was in the seat beside her, the expressionless aide stepped inside the limo, closed the door behind him, and sat in the corner facing them. He folded his hands in his lap and looked at the senator.

Senator Webb filled a second cup with coffee and placed it in front of Ben. Wisps of fragrant steam rose from both cups. "Cream and sugar, Mr. Dearinger?"

Ben's eyes narrowed to slits. "Keep your coffee. Just give me my son back."

The senator's eyebrows arched. "That's why we're here."

Tears filled Nikki's eyes. How could this…this *kidnapper* be so calm, so cold? She blinked, and the tears spilled over to run down her cheeks.

"Please, Senator. I'll do whatever you ask, I promise. Just don't hurt Joshua. He's only a baby. Please don't hurt him."

The expressive dark eyebrows drew together, separated by a deep crease. "I think there's been a misunderstanding." His glance slid sideways at his well-dressed assistant and then back to her. "You think I have your son?"

Nikki blinked. "You don't?"

Beside her, Ben leaned forward with a menacing glare. "I saw the list, Webb. I know what you've been up to. Don't mess with us."

"That again." The senator heaved a loud sigh. "That information has caused more trouble than you can possibly know." He looked from Ben to Nikki, realization dawning on his face. "You think it's real, don't you? You believe I'm being paid off by the Reynosa drug cartel."

Nikki studied him. He looked completely transparent and a little offended. She glanced at Ben, suddenly uncertain. Had Ben been mistaken in what he saw in that computer file?

Ben retreated slowly into the soft rear cushion, his gaze locked on Senator Webb, the confident cockiness gone from his expression. "You mean, it was a fake?"

"Of course it was a fake." The senator leaned forward, arms on his knees. "My entire political career has been devoted to stopping transcontinental criminal organizations like Reynosa. I'm an enthusiastic supporter of the Mérida Initiative, which provides practical tools to crack down on the appalling violence, the illegal weapons that flow from the U.S. into Mexico and the drugs that come across our southern border."

An image flashed into Nikki's mind—the men on the boat in Cozumel with wicked-looking guns clutched in their hands. Were they weapons from illegal arms dealers in the United States?

Ben shook his head. "So you're not on the Reynosa payroll?"

The senator straightened and held Ben's gaze. "I am not, nor have I ever been. I give you my word."

Nikki closed her eyes and tried to clear her thoughts. "Then do you know who has my son?"

"Oh, yes." Webb's smile was grim. "Not only that, I know where he's being held."

His assistant cleared his throat. "Senator, we should get going."

The senator nodded. "Of course. I'll explain on the way." He pressed a button in a console at his side. "We're ready, James."

A disembodied voice sounded from a speaker above Nikki's head. "Yes, sir."

"Where are we going?" Nikki asked.

Senator Webb smiled. "We're going to get your son back."

When the limo started to roll forward, the coffee in the cup in front of her sloshed. Nikki picked it up and gulped down the scalding liquid. Maybe the caffeine would still the whirling in her head. She wanted desperately to believe the man. He seemed sincere, especially when he spoke of stopping the drug cartels. And besides, he was a powerful senator. If she and Ben were going to get Joshua back safely, they needed all the help they could get.

TWENTY

Ben studied the senator through narrowed eyes. The senator's claim of innocence had the ring of truth. But Ben just couldn't believe the computer file that had caused him so much trouble over the past five months was a fake. He wasn't sure he *did* believe it. There were too many questions still unanswered. And topping the list was the most important.

"So if you're not responsible for kidnapping Joshua, who is?" he asked.

"This woman."

He nodded toward his assistant, who extracted a piece of paper from a briefcase at his feet and handed it to Ben.

A color snapshot depicted a woman in a long coat holding a child in her arms, a bulky overnight bag slung over her shoulder. The picture had been snapped as she exited an airport security checkpoint. Ben looked closely at the child. The photo was fuzzy, the features not quite clear but still discernable. Dark, curly hair, just like his. A slender face, like Nikki's, but the shape of the eyes, the nose, the chin—they were his in miniature. It was like looking at a baby picture of himself. His heart turned a crazy somersault.

My son. This is my son.

Nikki took the photo from his hands, tears streaming down her face. She looked at it and held it to her chest. "It's Allison, but she's wearing a blond wig."

"Her name is Alicia Strickland," the senator said.

Looking dazed, Nikki examined the photo again. "I don't understand. Isn't her name Allison Scott?"

The senator shook his head. "That's the name she assumed a little over four months ago, when she moved from Little Rock to Portland and took a job with the company where you work."

Ben couldn't believe his ears. The way Nikki talked about this woman, he'd assumed they had been friends for years. He turned a disbelieving stare her way. "You've only known her four months, and you didn't suspect anything when she *gave* you a time-share for a week?"

Nikki's face emptied of color. "She was new to town. Lonely. She didn't know anybody, and we hit it off immediately. She was just so…so nice."

Her stricken expression set off an ache inside Ben's chest. The guilt she must be feeling had to be agonizing. And here he was, being a jerk, trying to make her feel worse. He slid sideways to slip an arm around her and pull her close. "It's okay. She was working you, that's all. It wasn't your fault. Women make friends quicker than men."

"Mr. Dearinger's right." Senator Webb affirmed Ben's words with a nod. "The man who sent her there was counting on the fact that you'd befriend her. He'd discovered Mr. Dearinger's role in the disappearance of that computer file through his spy inside the Reynosa organization, and a little background work led him to you, my dear."

The hair on Ben's arm stood at attention. These people had discovered things about him that he didn't even know himself. Kind of creepy to know someone had investigated his background so thoroughly.

"If she doesn't work for you, then who sent her?" He watched Senator Webb closely, looking for any sign of deception as he answered.

A grim smile deepened the lines at the edges of the senator's mouth. "Have you ever heard of Robert Harlow?"

The name sounded familiar, but Ben couldn't place it. "Maybe."

"He's a politician, isn't he?" Nikki asked.

"That's right. He's a senator from Arkansas, and one of the front-runners to become our party's candidate in the next presidential election."

The connection dawned on Ben. "So are you. He's your competition."

The senator dipped his head, acknowledging the fact. "About eight months ago, certain members of my staff received word of a scheme to discredit me by leaking a false report to the press that I'm on the Reynosa cartel's payroll. The so-called proof was a chart that supposedly listed deposits into an untraceable bank account in Switzerland."

"The Cayman Islands," Ben corrected.

"Ah. That makes more sense, just for accessibility reasons." Senator Webb nodded at his aide, then continued. "It didn't take my people long to discover the existence of the data and the source. Harlow. His spy within the Reynosa organization was supposed to deliver a flash drive documenting the fake deposits to the news media in Mexico. Of course, news like that would immediately be relayed to media in the U.S. and plunge me into an instant scandal. Even when I was eventually cleared—and I would be—the damage would be done, my reputation tarnished."

"Wait a minute." The pieces were beginning to make sense to Ben. "Harlow's spy was Sergio Rueda."

"He was one of them, a minor player in the Reynosa cartel who thought he could make some money on the side. Unfortunately, the Reynosa people didn't take kindly to one of their own double-crossing them, or to an outsider like Harlow using them for his own purposes. They found out about the computer file, and Mr. Rueda was killed. But they failed to recover the flash drive." Webb stared at Ben. "Instead, you did."

"You said he was one of the spies inside the cartel." Nikki leaned forward, her expression intent. "There are others?"

"Of course. You know the saying. *There is no honor among thieves.* Many people in that organization think nothing of taking money in return for small, um, favors. The person who gave the file to Mr. Rueda also worked for Reynosa and was also on the take from Harlow. When the Reynosa cartel discovered his identity, they killed him, as well. News of his death in Mexico City was lost in the midst of the dozens of violent crimes that are perpetrated there every day." Webb glanced at his assistant. "Even I have an informant inside the cartel."

"You?" Ben asked. "Isn't that kind of unethical?"

The senator shifted in his seat, uncomfortable. "I've wrestled with that question. But you've got to understand. Information is power. The more you have, the more effective your decisions will be. If I know what's going on inside the Reynosa cartel, I can be more effective in my fight against them." He straightened. "In this case, my informant alerted me to the existence of that data file, and, as we followed the trail, it led to you."

Nikki glared at him. "So those two Reynosa thugs who assaulted us in Key West and again in Cozumel also worked for you?"

Bentley, the senator's aide, pulled another snapshot out of his briefcase. "Do you mean these men?"

Ben examined the photo the man handed him. Señor Mouth and the goon who strong-armed Nikki stood in front of a souvenir shop Ben recognized from Key West. He nodded and handed the photo to Nikki. "Yeah, that's them. They're your spies in the Reynosa cartel?"

"No, certainly not." Webb's denial was vehement. "Nor do they have any connection to the Reynosa organization. They work for Harlow, who apparently has realized his mistake in upsetting one of the most murderous criminal organizations in the world. He hired those two men to recover the lost flash drive."

Nikki looked at Ben. "And we thought they were Reynosa."

"I'll bet the ones on the boat in Cozumel were the real Reynosa," Ben said.

"Boat?" The senator looked from Ben to Nikki.

Either the man was a terrific actor, which was possible, or he really was telling the truth. He held their eyes without wavering. Ben's suspicions slipped a notch or two.

Ben filled him in on the incident in Cozumel, then nodded toward the photo. "Even if those two goons in Key West weren't from the Reynosa cartel, I'm guessing the men on the boat were. They were carrying assault rifles." He shook his head. "I don't understand one thing, though. Why did Reynosa want that computer file back so badly if it was a fake? I mean, if your reputation is ruined, surely that would be good for them since you're such a thorn in their sides."

Webb's shoulders jerked in a humorless laugh. "Because the information about me was fabricated, but the rest of it wasn't. Harlow's spy in Mexico City stole a real file and touched it up to implicate me. A smart move, actually. The real information would lend authenticity to the charges against me." He fell silent a moment, his gaze distant as he considered. "What I don't understand is why Alicia Strickland took your son last night. If the Reynosa men on that boat recovered the file, that would take you out of the equation. And you told Harlow's men that you gave the file to Reynosa, so he certainly knows it."

Nikki covered her mouth with both hands, her eyes wide. "I know why. Because I told Allison—I mean Alicia—that Ben has a copy." Her hands dropped like lead into her lap. "It's my fault."

The senator's gaze slid sideways to lock on Ben. "Is it true? Do you have a copy of the computer file?"

Ben returned the senator's stare while a silent battle raged in his mind. Could they trust this guy? Sure, he looked honest, but that might be a ruse. After all, he was a politician. This convoluted story could all be a load of garbage, meant to convince them of his innocence just so Ben would turn over the only proof he had. The only leverage he had to negotiate the return of his son.

Okay, heavenly Dad, if You're really out there and ready to help us, I could use some advice here. I don't want to do the wrong thing.

He searched the senator's face. Gradually, like water

seeping into a sponge, a decision crept over him. Without looking away from Senator Webb's eyes, he slipped
his camera out of his pocket, slid open the catch to a
compartment on the side, and popped out the SD card.
He offered it to the senator on the palm of his hand.

Webb took it with a grateful smile. "Thank you for
your trust." He handed the card to his assistant. "Bentley,
let's take a look."

Bentley, who had remained stoic and silent throughout
most of the conversation, extracted a laptop computer
from the briefcase. When he lifted the lid and pressed a
series of buttons, the screen flashed to life. He slid the
SD card into a slot in the computer's side.

"You took a picture of the file?" he asked Ben, his
fingers busy on the keyboard.

Ben shook his head. "No, I made an actual copy of
the spreadsheet. An SD card is just a storage device,
exactly like a flash drive. But a digital camera doesn't
recognize the format, so when you view pictures through
the camera's screen, the file is invisible. You need a
computer to access it."

Senator Webb looked impressed. "Nice job. I would
never have thought of that."

They watched the screen while Bentley displayed the
contents of the SD card. Nikki grabbed Ben's hand. Hers
was so icy, he sandwiched it between his and tried to
rub some warmth into it. How was she holding up? He
glanced at her face. Pale and worried, but not panicky.

Bentley double clicked on the computer file and the
spreadsheet software opened. A second later, the data
loaded. Row after row of numbers and dates, none of
them formatted.

"Notice the tabs." Ben pointed at the bottom of the screen. "There are two sheets."

The first tab, the one they were seeing, was labeled *Depósitos*. Deposits. Bentley clicked the tab for the second sheet, the one labeled *Cuentas*. Accounts.

At the top of the page were the names and addresses of several offshore banks in the Cayman Islands, along with what was clearly an electronic routing number. Beneath each bank's listing were two columns containing a name and another number.

"That number is an account number," Ben told them. "It matches the number on the first page. So sheet number one records deposits made to specific bank accounts, and the second identifies the bank account's owner."

Bentley scrolled down. A few names were English, but most Spanish. Ben didn't recognize any of them, though a glance at the senator's serious expression hinted that he did. Then they came to the name that had caused all the trouble.

Senator Adam Webb. The senator closed his eyes and shook his head slowly, his lips a hard, grim line.

The limo rolled to a stop and the driver's voice came over the loudspeaker. "This is as close as they'll let us get, sir."

"Thank you, James." The senator looked at Ben and then Nikki. "Let's go get your son back."

TWENTY-ONE

Nikki slid across the leather seat and followed Ben out of the limo. She grasped his hand as they waited for the senator and Mr. Bentley to join them in the frigid morning air. The sun had not yet risen above the jagged mountain peaks in the east, but the sky cast a chilly light on the restaurant parking lot where they stood. A dim lamp shone from somewhere inside the building, but there was no movement. It was still several hours before the restaurant opened for lunch.

A row of cars lined the opposite edge of the parking lot, several with streams of exhaust rising into the cold air from the tailpipes. A cluster of men, all in dark coats and gloves, stood behind one of the vehicles. Another man leaned against the side of the building, looking around the corner at a hotel next door.

A man broke away from the group and approached. He nodded in deference to Senator Webb.

"Senator, I'm Special Agent Farmer. I'm in charge of this operation."

Nikki restrained herself from flying at the man. "Where's my son?" Her sense of urgency colored her voice and made it come out shrill. She clung to Ben, shivering.

"These are the boy's parents," Senator Webb told the agent. "Could you give us an update on the situation?"

"Here, ma'am. Put this on." The agent took off his coat. He handed it to Ben, who draped the heavy garment around her shoulders, and he wound the agent's warm wool scarf around her neck.

"Th-thank you," she said.

Farmer addressed the senator, but glanced at Ben and Nikki to include them in his update. "We lost track of her for a while after she took the boy from his grandmother's house."

Nikki gasped. "Mom! I forgot to call her back. She must be worried sick."

"There's an agent at her house in Portland, ma'am. We're keeping her updated. The local police activated the Amber Alert system as soon as they got her call, and we placed someone there for her protection." He glanced at Senator Webb. "If what you told the director on the phone is true, sir, we're not taking any chances with the safety of anyone who might be able to offer testimony in the trial."

"I promise you, it's true." The senator nodded toward Ben. "I hope we have enough proof now to implicate Harlow."

"Wait a minute," Ben said. "What do you mean you *lost track of her?* Were you watching her before she kidnapped Joshua?"

"Not physically," Farmer said. "We received a call from Senator Webb's office yesterday, alerting us to the fact that she was a suspicious person living under an assumed identity, along with an urgent request to monitor her cell phone. If we'd known what she intended, of course we would have been on-site to stop her." His gaze switched to Nikki. "We intercepted the phone call you made to her last night."

"That's how we knew where you were," Mr. Bentley told them. "You said you were staying with friends who run a church. That gave us a clue. Most of the churches on the island are Catholic, run by Catholic priests. There aren't many run by individuals, so finding the right one was fairly easy."

Nikki managed a weak laugh. "Allison mentioned the possibility that my mother's phone might be tapped, and all the while, hers was."

A sympathetic smile appeared on Mr. Bentley's normally expressionless face. "I listened to the replay of that call. She told you about a possible tap on your mother's phone to keep you from saying that she was coming to get them both. Remember, she suggested that you only say your friend was coming to help out. That way your mother wouldn't question her suggestion about taking the child alone."

And I fell for it. I followed her instructions to the letter. Nikki closed her eyes, guilt pounding inside her skull.

Agent Farmer continued. "Immediately after she hung up with you, she placed several calls to a private number in Arkansas, and we've traced that phone to one of Senator Harlow's aides. Her calls weren't answered, though. The next thing we heard was from the emergency dispatcher reporting the kidnapping."

"How did she get here?" Ben's gesture swept their surroundings. "Salt Lake City is a long way from Portland."

"When she picked up the child, she went straight to the airport and bought a ticket to Seattle under the name

Allison Scott. The kidnapping hadn't been reported yet, so no one knew to watch for her. In Seattle, she left the security area, reentered a few minutes later wearing different clothes and a wig and purchased a flight to Salt Lake under the name Alicia Strickland. She and the child arrived here just after midnight last night and took a taxi to this hotel." He pointed toward the building on the opposite side of the restaurant. "They haven't left. We hacked into the hotel's computer system and discovered a woman named Julia Pritchard rented room 511 around twelve-thirty. She paid cash for one night and requested a crib. That couldn't have been a coincidence, so we're positive it's her."

"Why are we standing here?" Nikki wanted to shout, but she kept her tone reasonable. "Why aren't you going in there to get them?"

"Ma'am, we're waiting for the go-ahead from D.C. When that happens, and as soon as our hostage negotiator arrives, we'll evacuate the hotel."

"Evacuate the hotel?" Ben's arm around her tightened. "That will take forever."

"We need to ensure the safety of everyone, sir." Farmer dipped his head toward the nearby limo. "Why don't you all wait in there, where it's warmer? I'll keep you posted."

Nikki's mind stumbled over the words *hostage negotiator.* Several movies she'd seen that featured hostage negotiators came to mind, along with bloody scenes of failed rescues.

No. Not my son. Not Joshua.

She had to do something.

* * *

Agent Farmer's cell phone rang. "Excuse me a moment."

He stepped away to answer the call.

Ben addressed Senator Webb. "Listen, I understand about keeping innocent people safe and all, but this is our son we're talking about. A two-year-old boy. He's been in the custody of this crazy woman for over twelve hours now. Can't something be done to hurry this along?"

"I know you're concerned, Mr. Dearinger. We all are." The senator's glance swept the agents clustered at the other end of the building. "These men represent the best the federal government has to offer. We need to trust them."

Yeah, right. Ben scoffed at the idea. *Trust the government. That's a good one.*

But he couldn't very well express his disdain to Senator Webb, who was a member of that same government.

"I understand that, but you're a senator. Surely you can throw your weight around, get things moving."

The senator laughed. "I don't have much weight with the director of the FBI."

"I know, but—"

"Senator Webb?" Special Agent Farmer turned and extended the phone in their direction. "Sir, if you don't mind, the director would like to speak with you. He wants to verify a few facts we learned from your staff."

"Of course." To Ben, he said, "I'll do my best to speed things along." The senator clapped a hand on Ben's bare arm. "You're not dressed for this cold, Mr. Dearinger. Agent Farmer is right. Why don't you wait in the limousine with Ms. Hoffman while I speak with the director? I'll join you both in a minute."

He walked toward the special agent, Mr. Bentley trailing behind him.

Ben turned toward Nikki. "Well, maybe now we'll—"

He stopped. Nikki was gone.

TWENTY-TWO

Nikki ran as quietly as she could across the parking lot and around the side of the hotel. Every second, she expected to hear angry voices ordering her to stop. They did not come. She dashed to the cover of a tall hedge, then slipped around the corner of the hotel. Only when she could no longer see the restaurant did she stop to get her bearings. She collapsed against the wall, her breath coming hard. The agent assigned to watch the hotel was focused on the front entrance. From his vantage point on the opposite corner of the restaurant, he couldn't see the back of the building.

A quick scan of the small parking lot showed that his surveillance was probably sufficient to spot anyone leaving the hotel. Bordered by a tall concrete fence, there was only one row for parking cars, and the only way a car could go in or out was on the side of the building that faced the restaurant.

But the front wasn't the only way into the building. As she knew there would be, there was a back exit.

What am I doing? I should let the FBI handle this.

But that was *her* son in there, being held captive by a woman who had deceived her. Remorse twisted her stomach into a knot, so strong it nearly doubled her over. She had been so stupid, so gullible. How could she have fallen for Allison's lies? Ben was right. Who was dumb enough to believe that someone she barely knew would be generous enough to give her a week in a Florida resort, free of charge?

Snatches of conversations she'd had with Allison over the past four months came back to her. She'd been such a sucker, pouring out her life story to her new friend. Everything, all the intimate details. Her college crushes. Ben.

She used me to get details about Ben. Then she sent me down there to be kidnapped by those men, to force Ben to hand over that file. I fell for her lies—and now my baby is in danger. Oh, Joshua! Mommy's so sorry.

Nikki was all Joshua had. Mom had always been there to help, but Nikki's son was her responsibility. He depended on her for security, for protection. And she'd let him down.

Well, I'm going to get him back if I have to tear her into little, tiny pieces to do it.

Her teeth set together, Nikki jogged to the building's rear door. Inside, she found herself in a stairwell. The slamming of the door echoed upward, a hollow sound that drifted to the unseen floors above her. Room 511, the agent had said. She hadn't stopped to count the rows of windows, but the building couldn't be much taller than five floors. She started to climb.

On the third floor, she realized she was sweating, both from the heat and the stress of what lay ahead. How would she get Joshua away from Allison? Could she lure her into the hallway, knock her out with a heavy object?

Nikki shed the coat and scarf. They were slowing

her down. She draped them over the handrail, and continued her upward trek.

Ben dashed to the limousine. In the front seat, the driver bent over to fiddle with the controls on the radio. Ben ignored him and jerked open the rear door. His stomach plummeted to his feet.

Nikki was not inside.

The front window slid down. "Are you looking for the young lady, sir?"

Ben whirled toward the driver. "Yes. Did you see where she went?"

Even as he asked the question, Ben knew the answer. There was only one place she *would* go.

The driver pointed at the hotel. "She went over to the hotel a minute ago, around the back. Seemed in a hurry. I figured she had to use the…uh, you know. Facilities."

Ben wanted to shout at the man, to ask why he'd let her go. Then he realized—the driver had no idea what was going on here. He was probably a local chauffeur, hired by the senator's staff to meet the jet at the airport and cart the important politician around town. If he'd been a driver for any length of time, he was used to minding his own business and not asking questions.

Ben plastered what he hoped was a casual smile on his face. "All right. Thanks. I think I'll go find her."

"Yes, sir." The window swept upward.

Ben glanced at the dark-suited FBI agents behind him. Five or six stood in a small group, talking and throwing surreptitious glances at the senator, who still held the cell phone up to his ear. Farmer and Bentley both stood nearby, their backs to Ben. The agent at the far corner of the building kept watch on the hotel entrance.

Ben walked casually out of view, in the direction of the hedge separating the restaurant from the hotel. He wasn't about to stand here and let Nikki face a kidnapper alone. If anyone tried to stop him, they'd have a fight on their hands.

TWENTY-THREE

On the top floor, Nikki peeked through the narrow window in a heavy door marked with a large black five. She saw no movement, nothing but an elevator. Moving quietly, she slipped inside and paused to get her bearings.

She stood in the center of a hallway, in a wide alcove. A set of elevator doors faced her. Thin maroon carpet covered the floor and matched the narrow stripes on the wallpaper. A faint musty odor spoke of the hotel's age, or perhaps the inattentiveness of the cleaning staff. A sign on the wall beside her indicated the numbers of the rooms to the left and right. She turned left and crept down the hall.

A noise sent her stomach leaping into her throat. She jerked to a halt, then identified the source. Behind her, in the opposite direction, an opening in the wall led to a vending area. The noise she'd heard was the tumble of ice inside an ice machine. Willing her pulse to slow, she continued.

Room 511 lay midway down the corridor, on the left. Nikki leaned against the wall beside it. How could she get in that room? No way could she break down the door. She wasn't nearly strong enough. Besides, Allison had probably bolted it. Could she trick her way in? This hotel wasn't the caliber to have room service. Besides, anyone who'd ever watched television would recognize that ploy.

Nikki had no ideas, no options. There was only one thing to do. She had to reason with her son's kidnapper.

She stepped up to the door and banged on it with her fist. "Allison, it's me. Open this door."

No response.

She pounded again. "Allison, open up this instant. I want my son."

"Nikki?" Allison's voice, muffled through the thick wood. "What are you doing here? How did you find me?"

"Never mind that. I'm here to get Joshua. Open up."

A moan. "Oh, no. They've found me, haven't they? The police."

Nikki laid her ear to the door. Allison sounded upset, near tears. That could work to her advantage. Maybe she could scare her into giving up. "Yes, they've found you. There are FBI agents all over the place."

"Nooooo." A definite sob. "I didn't mean for this to happen."

"Then open the door. Give me Joshua and maybe they'll go easy on you."

"Are you alone?"

Hope swelled in her chest. She was going to get inside. "I am. I promise. Everyone else is outside."

Another sob, and then a sound. The dead bolt slid open. Nikki backed up and raised her hands in front of her. The moment that door cracked open, she'd rush it, smash it into Allison and overpower her while she was still dazed from the attack.

But what if she's carrying Joshua? I might hurt him.

She let her hands drop.

The door opened a crack, just barely, and then several seconds passed before she heard Allison's voice from farther inside the room.

"You can come in."

Moving with caution, Nikki laid her palm on the door and pushed it open. Slowly.

She stepped inside a standard hotel room. The bathroom door to her right stood open. To her left, a closet alcove with an empty clothes bar hung beneath a shelf containing an iron and an extra pillow. In front of her, two double beds faced a low dresser. A television set hung from the ceiling on a metal frame. Allison stood between the beds, holding—

"Joshua!" Nikki's throat squeezed shut. Joshua's head lay across Allison's shoulder, his arms and legs dangling. His eyes were closed, his little face peaceful in sleep.

She held her arms out. "Give him to me."

"Not yet," Allison replied.

Nikki took a step toward them. She'd pry her child out of that woman's arms if she had to.

But then Allison twisted her body sideways, and Nikki froze. Allison held a pair of scissors in her right hand, the sharp point poised next to the baby's chubby neck.

Nikki's heart slammed to a stop. "You—you wouldn't hurt him." Her statement became a plea. "Would you?"

"I don't want to hurt him, you know I don't."

Nikki shook her head, unable to tear her gaze away from the scissors. "I don't know anything about you, Allison. Or, Alicia."

Alicia's eyes widened. "They know who I am?"

Nikki nodded, but all her attention was focused on her son. Something was wrong. He hadn't moved at all. Joshua was a light sleeper. The sound of her voice should have woken him.

"What's wrong with him? What have you done to him?"

"Nothing's wrong." Alicia hefted the child farther up on her shoulder. His limp limbs flopped. "I gave him something to make him stop crying, that's all. We both needed to get some sleep."

Horror crept over Nikki. "You *drugged* him?"

"It was just Benadryl. He'll be fine."

Every muscle in Nikki's body strained with tension. When she got hold of that, that baby thief, she'd strangle her with her bare hands. But first, she had to get Joshua safely away from her.

"Are there really FBI agents outside?" Alicia cast a nervous glance toward the window.

"Yes. A bunch of them."

"And they know what room I'm in?"

Nikki nodded. "They know every move you've made since you kidnapped Joshua."

Alicia winced. "Kidnapped. I can't believe this is happening." The scissors trembled as her fingers tightened on the handle. "I've got to get out of here." Nikki stood still as Alicia's gaze darted in a circle around the room. "Okay, here's what we're going to do. Back up."

"What?"

"I said, back up. Into the bathroom."

She's going to leave with Joshua.

"Allison." She stumbled over the name. "Or Alicia, or whoever you are, listen to me. Just give Joshua to me. If you return him safely, it won't go so badly for you. But if you hurt him—"

She swallowed, unwilling to consider the possibility of Joshua being hurt.

The scissors circled the baby's neck to press against the back, the tip resting at the soft part of his skull. "Do it, Nikki."

Nikki backed away, her eyes on the madwoman who held her son. Alicia moved forward. The scissors moved away for an instant, long enough for Alicia to scoop up her purse from the dresser and sling it over her free shoulder, then returned to their menacing position. Nikki backed into the bathroom.

"Now close the door."

Nikki hesitated for only a second. Alicia had the upper hand. She had Joshua. Nikki closed the bathroom door.

A minute later, she heard the outside door slam. Alicia was escaping with her son! Nikki jerked both doors open and dashed into the hallway in time to see Alicia's back and the top of Joshua's curly hair disappear around the corner, toward the elevators. She ran after them and arrived in time to see the fire door slam shut.

Ben slipped inside the back door. Ahead of him, a fire door led to the hotel's main level, but he knew Nikki hadn't gone there. She'd heard the room number as well as him. Joshua was being held on the fifth floor, and that's where Nikki would have gone. Ben dashed up the stairs, taking them two at a time.

On the third floor, he stopped. A dark coat and scarf lay draped over the handrail. The same ones Special Agent Farmer gave Nikki to wear. He picked up the scarf.

If anything happens to Nikki…

He crushed the wool in his fist and buried his face in it. The years since she left him had been empty. Dull. Sure, he'd managed to duck any responsibilities beyond guiding the next group of tourists on a scuba dive, which was exactly what he always said he wanted. No ties. No encumbrances. He could go where he chose, do whatever he wished, answer to no one but himself. It was the life he'd planned, the one Dad had led. Following in his father's footsteps had created a sort of invisible bond between them, a bond that Ben had desperately wanted as a young boy.

But in the past several days, from the moment he saw Nikki again on the dock in Key West, he'd begun to realize that wasn't the life he wanted after all. He wanted more.

He wanted Nikki and Joshua.

Still clutching the scarf, Ben placed a foot on the next step. A sound stopped him.

From somewhere above him, somewhere close, a door slammed shut. The noise echoed down the stairwell, followed by footsteps. Someone was coming.

An instant later, the door slammed again. His pulse kicked up a notch at the sound of Nikki's voice.

"Alicia, stop right there!"

TWENTY-FOUR

"Please, don't do this." Nikki stood one flight above, her hand on the rail, and looked down to the next landing at the woman who held her son. "I can't believe you'd really hurt Joshua. You're…" She swallowed. "You're not the kind of person who would hurt a child."

A tortured expression twisted Alicia's features. "Like you said a minute ago, you don't know me. You don't know what kind of person I am."

"There's a lot I don't know." Nikki edged down one step. One step closer to her baby. "But surely everything you told me wasn't a lie. You told me about your childhood, and your first prom. Those were real memories, weren't they?"

Alicia hesitated, then nodded. "Those were real."

Nikki took another step. She was just ten steps away from them now. "Whatever brought you to Portland, whatever reason you had for coming there, we became friends, didn't we?"

The woman ran a tongue quickly around her lips. Her eyes darted down the stairs. Nikki didn't move, lest she frighten her into running farther away.

I've got to keep her talking, distract her. If I can just get close enough to grab those scissors…

"I know why you lied to me," Nikki said. "You were just doing what you'd been told to do. Maybe even paid to do?"

Alicia's head jerked up and down. "I needed the money. I've got college loans to pay off and credit cards and rent. I wasn't making enough money as a low-level secretary on Senator Harlow's staff. The bank was about to repossess my car. So when his aide approached me with this assignment, I jumped at it."

Nikki eased herself down one more step. "But you didn't know it would end up like this, did you?"

A near hysterical laugh escaped Alicia's lips. "Are you kidding? They got me that job as a receptionist at your company, and I was supposed to become your friend. Get you to talk about your ex-boyfriend. I was supposed to find out if he was still in contact with you. That's all."

"That doesn't sound so terrible." Nikki took another step.

Alicia brandished the scissors, pointed them at the base of the baby's skull. "Stop right there, Nikki. I'm not kidding. I don't want to hurt him, but—" Her chest heaved with a dry sob. "Nothing has turned out like it was supposed to."

She dashed forward, down the next set of stairs. Terror gripped Nikki for an instant. *I can't lose them.*

She leaped down the stairs after them, screaming, "Alicia, stop! Don't take him away."

Alicia came to a halt on the next landing. When she turned, her eyes were bright with tears. "'Just make friends with her,' he said. 'Let me know if her boyfriend sends her anything.'" She gave a short, high-pitched

laugh. "Yeah, at first that was all. But then he wanted
me to get you and the kid down to Key West."

Nikki paused. "Senator Harlow wanted us both in
Key West?"

Sniffing, Alicia nodded. "When we realized Ben
didn't know anything about Joshua, Harlow wanted to
confront him. You know, shock him. They'd use Joshua
as leverage to get that stupid computer file back. But no."
A poisonous glare covered the distance between them.
"You had to leave the kid at home. I tried to get you to
take him, but you wanted a vacation alone."

Nikki swallowed. She remembered that conversation,
how Allison/Alicia kept suggesting that Joshua would
fall in love with the ocean. Actually, that argument had
been the deciding factor in Nikki taking her mother's
suggestion to use the vacation as a much-needed break
from the stresses of single parenthood. Ben's love for
a carefree life near the ocean had kept him from her.
Irrationally, Nikki didn't want to expose Joshua to that
lifestyle, not yet. She didn't want to share her son with
the ocean.

"But why not just tell Ben about Joshua?" Nikki
remembered the picture in Key West. "Why not just
send him a picture?"

"Don't you think I tried that?" Alicia's voice rose
into a near shout. "I have tons of pictures of you two, but
Harlow wouldn't go for it. He wanted the shock value of
a confrontation."

She stood in the center of the landing, her back to the
fourth floor door. Her voice rose higher in pitch every
minute as hysteria crept closer. She kept swinging the
arm that held the scissors as she spoke, but the deadly
point always returned to Joshua's skull. Looking down

on her, Nikki's mind was a frantic jumble of fear. If Alicia became hysterical, she might hurt Joshua accidentally. But how to calm her down?

And then, Nikki saw something. Hope flared like a beacon inside her.

Nikki's words echoed down the stairwell. Ben jerked his head upward. An unfamiliar voice answered. Alicia Strickland. They were above him.

What could he do? The conversation continued above his head. He half listened, his brain searching desperately for a plan. Could he sneak up the stairs, maybe get close enough to grab Joshua and run with him? A possibility, but first he had to know exactly where the women were.

He took a step up.

Rubber from his flip-flop flapped against his heel, and he halted, straining his ears. Did they hear the noise above? No, apparently not. Their conversation continued without a pause. But these flip-flops he'd gotten from the donation box in Mexico weren't conducive to silent movement. He slipped them off, and continued to inch upward.

"Nothing has turned out like it was supposed to."

The cry, followed by a flurry of footsteps, sent Ben scurrying backward. Alicia was running down the stairs, directly toward him. From the conversation he was hearing, he surmised the woman had Joshua, and Nikki was following her. She kept pleading for Alicia not to hurt the baby. Did the kidnapper have a weapon? He couldn't act until he knew.

The sound of footsteps stopped, and the conversation continued. Ben once again crept forward, silent on bare feet, until he was half a floor below them. Cautiously, his movements slow, he leaned sideways to peer around the stairs.

One glimpse was all he needed. He jerked back. Alicia stood on the fourth floor landing, the next one up, her back to the door. Judging from Nikki's voice, she was apparently not far above Alicia. A plan began to form in Ben's mind.

As silently as he could, he backed away. He picked up the discarded scarf from the third floor, then continued, all the way down to the second floor. Then, with slow movements that wouldn't make any noise at all, he opened the fire door and entered the hotel corridor. The door closed behind him with a quiet *snick*.

There was probably another stairwell in this building somewhere, but he didn't have time to look for it. He dashed across the hallway and stabbed at the elevator button.

After an interminably long wait, the doors whooshed open. A boy stood inside. The kid's gaze swept downward, took in the shorts and bare feet, the wool scarf, and then came back to rest on Ben's face.

Ben rushed into the elevator, and the kid backed up to stand against the rear wall, as far away from him as the small space allowed. Ben punched the button for the fourth floor, and noticed that the fifth floor light glowed. The kid was going up, presumably back to his room. When the doors closed, he examined the boy. Around ten, maybe.

"Hey, kid, I need a favor."

The boy's face darkened with suspicion. "What kind of favor?"

"I need you to go back downstairs and over to the

restaurant next door. There's a bunch of men hanging around the parking lot. Tell them this—*Alicia and the boy are in the stairwell on the fourth floor.* Can you remember that?"

The boy shook his head. "My mom only gave me permission to go down to the game room by the lobby until I ran out of quarters. Then I hafta go back to our room."

Ben reached into his pocket. He pulled out the money Thomas had given him in Cozumel and flipped through the bills. The smallest was a twenty. He peeled it off and held it out to the kid.

"You know how many quarters there are in twenty bucks? Eighty. All for one little favor."

The boy didn't take his eyes off the bill, but he shook his head again. "I'll get in trouble if I leave the building."

Ben peeled off another twenty. "Please. It's important. If you get in trouble, I'll talk to your mom for you."

A second of hesitation, and then the kid snatched the two bills out of his hand. "You got a deal, mister."

A tone sounded. The display above the door announced their arrival at the fourth floor.

He glanced at the kid. "Don't forget. *Alicia and the boy are in the stairwell on the fourth floor.* And hurry."

The boy nodded. Ben crouched low. When the doors slid apart, he crept, bent double, into the hallway. He didn't move until the elevator and the boy were gone, then he inched toward the stairwell fire door.

Please don't let her turn around and see me.

The prayer streamed from his thoughts automatically.

His son needed help from him, and he needed help from his heavenly Dad.

He braced his hands on the doorjamb and inched his head upward to the narrow window.

TWENTY-FIVE

Nikki's gaze locked with Ben's through the glass.

He's right behind her. If he jumps through that door, he might be able to grab her from behind.

But if Ben startled her, she might hurt Joshua. Nikki's chest squeezed so tight she couldn't force a breath into her lungs. She had to let Ben know about the scissors before he did anything.

"Wait!" She held her palm flat toward Alicia, and prayed Ben would know she was really talking to him.

Alicia's brow creased. "What?"

Nikki lowered her hand. "I mean, wait a minute. I just thought of something. If Senator Harlow told you to kidnap Joshua, then he's ultimately responsible, isn't he? He'll get in far more trouble than you." Her foot moved in an automatic attempt to continue getting closer to her son, but she stopped herself before she took the step. She couldn't take a chance on doing anything to make Alicia run farther away. "Unless you hurt him. Then nothing is going to stop you from going to jail, Alicia."

Alicia's skin emptied of color. Panic widened her eyes. "I can't go to jail." As Nikki hoped, she swung the hand holding the scissors wide to emphasize her words. "I can't!"

Behind Alicia, Ben lifted his fingers to the window. He formed a circle with his forefinger and thumb, the scuba signal for "okay."

Thank goodness. He sees the scissors. She didn't dare look directly at him, for fear of alerting Alicia to his presence.

At that moment, Joshua moved. His legs jerked, and he lifted his head. It wobbled a minute, then collapsed back onto Alicia's shoulder. Her son's soft whine twisted Nikki's heart in her chest.

Behind Alicia, the door handle edged downward. Ben was unlatching the door.

Nikki raised her voice to a near shout. She had to try to drown out any sound Ben might make. "Maybe you can work out a deal with the FBI. You testify against Senator Harlow, and they'll give you a reduced sentence. Maybe even dismiss all the charges. I don't know how that works, but if you give Joshua back unharmed, maybe they'll do that."

"You don't understand!" Alicia screamed the words. The scissors swung wildly. "Harlow told me to keep an eye on both of you. When you called and said Ben had given the computer file to the Reynosa people but that he had a copy, I tried to call Harlow. That weasel wouldn't take my calls. I had to do something, didn't I? Harlow can use this kid to get Ben's copy." She clutched Joshua tighter, and the child whined again.

Behind her, the door swung outward without a sound. Just a few inches.

"So you decided to kidnap Joshua on your own?" Nikki shook her head. "Alicia, why would you do that?"

"Because I didn't know what else to do." She punctuated her shout with a stamp of her foot. "I'm sick of this job. I'm going to rent a car and drive him to Arkansas and let Harlow deal with it." Her arm swung wide again. "And while I'm there, I'm going to tell him I quit!"

Several things happened in the next instant.

A deep voice blasted up the stairwell from below. "Alicia Strickland, this is the FBI. We know you have the child. Bring him down now, and you won't be harmed."

Alicia's hand, the one holding the scissors, froze in the extended position. Her panic-stricken eyes darted from Nikki to the lower staircase.

The door behind her burst fully open. Ben rushed forward, a gray scarf in his hands. Quick as a flash, he looped the scarf over the arm with the scissors and jerked.

The scissors flew out of her hand, bounced off the wall and clattered to the floor.

At exactly that moment, Joshua reared backward, groggy and wailing. His legs and arms kicked against his captor. With her other arm entangled in the scarf, Alicia couldn't hold him.

For one heart-stopping moment, Nikki watched her son teeter in the loose grip of his kidnapper.

He's going to fall backward down the stairs. He'll be killed!

A scream tore from her throat as she leaped toward him, arms outstretched.

She was not in time.

But Ben was. He gave the scarf a vicious jerk that twisted Alicia halfway around toward him and scooped up the little boy with his free arm.

TWENTY-SIX

"Ma'am, do you have any idea how reckless your actions were? You don't know what a desperate kidnapper might do." Puffs of white streamed from Special Agent Farmer's nostrils. Combined with the fierce scowl, his face resembled that of an angry bull.

Nikki hugged Joshua close beneath the heavy coat. Chubby arms wrapped around her neck, and his warm body snuggled against her. She rested her cheek on his soft dark curls and smiled at the agent.

Ben's arm tightened around them. "You don't know what a desperate mother might do to rescue her child, Agent Farmer."

Senator Webb clapped the agent on the back. "It all worked out and you didn't even have to fire a shot. The director will be pleased about that."

Nikki glanced across the parking lot, where Alicia sat in the backseat of the Salt Lake County patrol car. Her head drooped forward, and hair streamed down to hide her face. "What will happen to her?"

The senator followed her gaze. "I'm not sure. The federal prosecutor might cut a deal with her if she'll testify against Harlow. We probably have enough evidence against him for a conviction, but her testimony would cinch the deal. Still, she'll do some time. Kidnapping is a serious crime, and especially since she took your son across state lines."

Nikki tried to muster some sympathy for her former friend, but failed. The woman had threatened Joshua's life. Whatever sentence she received would be fully justified and probably not nearly enough.

Three people approached. A young boy and his parents. The boy's shoulders slumped as he held two twenty-dollar bills toward Ben.

"My mom and dad said I should give this back." His voice sounded reconciled, but not very happy. "On account of I'm not supposed to get paid for doing a good deed."

Grinning, Ben shook his head. "Nope. A deal's a deal. I'm not taking it back. You helped save my son's life."

The boy raised hopeful eyes toward his father, who, after a slight hesitation, nodded.

Grinning, the kid shoved the money back in his pocket and turned an impish look on Ben. "If you'da just told me there was a kidnapping going on and FBI agents and a senator—" his eyes gleamed as he eyed the shiny black limo "—I woulda done it for free."

Ben laughed. "I'll remember that next time."

When the trio headed toward the hotel, Joshua began a groggy wail. "I want my mommy."

Nikki snuggled him close. "Mommy's here, baby. You're safe now." She looked up at Ben. "You were amazing in there."

Ben shook his head. "*You* were amazing." He ran a hand over his son's soft curls as the little eyes closed again. "I wish you had told me."

The sound of regret in his whisper sent a wave of

guilt washing over her. "I'm so sorry. I shouldn't have left the way I did, I see that now. I was so afraid you would think I was trying to trap you, to saddle you with a responsibility you never wanted."

He stepped in front of her and looked down into her eyes. "I didn't know what I wanted. I was too busy trying to emulate my father, because—" He ran a hand over his eyes. "I don't know. Maybe in a weird way I was trying to make him proud of me by being like him. But I don't want to be like him anymore. And I don't want my son to grow up without a dad, like I did."

Nikki searched his face. Did he mean it? Did she dare hope? "You don't?"

"No." His gaze became gentle. "And I don't want to spend another day without you, either. I love you, Nikki."

Joy rushed through her heart. Oh, how she had longed to hear those words. Her eyes burred with unshed tears. "I love you, too. I've never stopped loving you."

"Then tell me something. Why'd you sneak in there on your own? Why didn't you tell me, so we could go together?"

"Oh, Ben, I don't know if I can explain it." Nikki leaned against the limousine and tried to piece the fragments of her thoughts together. Her fears. Her guilt. "I'm a good mother, I really am, but this was my fault, my stupidity. I put Joshua in danger." Nikki rested her forehead on her son's head. "He's my responsibility. From before he was born, I'm the one who's taken care of him, and protected him, and kept him safe." She looked into Ben's eyes and tried to pour the depth of her feelings into her words. "Don't you understand? I'm all he has."

Ben's arms came around her, pulled her and Joshua

into a firm embrace. He pressed a gentle kiss on Joshua's head, and then buried his face in her hair. His breath warmed her ear.

"Not anymore." His words held a promise, a vow. "Not anymore."

EPILOGUE

Ben fiddled with his tie, his fingers clumsily twisting the fabric this way and that. Why did these things have to be so complicated? He should have gone with the clip-on. When he finished, he inspected his work in the mirror and then, disgusted, ripped it apart to try again. He couldn't go to his own wedding with a lopsided tie.

A knock sounded on the door. "How are you doing in there?"

He turned to see Pastor Thomas step into the room. He and Denise flew in from Cozumel last night. "I'm glad to see you. Think you can give me a hand with this?"

The tall man chuckled. "It's been a while, but I think I remember how." He grasped the silken ends and twisted expertly. "I heard a news report on the way here I thought you might find interesting. The grand jury in Little Rock just handed down an indictment against Senator Robert Harlow for fraud, embezzlement and conspiracy to commit murder."

"I'm not surprised." Ben turned once again toward the mirror and checked his reflection. "Nikki and I had to fly down there last week to testify."

Between the grand jury hearings for Senator Harlow

and the one for Alicia Strickland last month, both he and Nikki had lost several days of work. Plus, they'd have to go back for the trials. But they'd do whatever it took to put those two behind bars. Thankfully, his boss at the water sports store where he'd gotten a job was an understanding guy.

The door opened again, and a small tornado whirled into the room. "Daddy, Daddy!"

A thrill shot through Ben as he caught Joshua up in his arms. Would he ever get tired of hearing that name on his son's lips? "Hey, big guy. Aren't you supposed to be with Grandma?"

"Yes, he is." Nikki's mother appeared in the doorway, a frazzled expression on her face. "I just turned around for a second and he was gone. Joshua, come with me. We've got a special seat in the front row."

Displaying a stubborn streak every bit as strong as Nikki's, Joshua's arms tightened around Ben's neck. "I don't wanna leave my daddy!"

And Daddy doesn't want to leave you either, buddy.

Ben smiled at Nikki's mother. "Go ahead and sit down. I'll keep him with me." He hugged his son tight. "After all, I can't get married without my best man at my side, can I?"

For the rest of her life, whenever she recalled her wedding day, Nikki would always remember the scent of the roses from her bouquet, the smooth feel of silk as it brushed against her legs and the glow of love in her husband's eyes.

They stood in front of the altar in their church sanctuary, joined by a small group of friends to witness the exchange of their vows. As the minister instructed Ben and Nikki to face one another, she glanced at the others turned their way. Twenty or so guests were scattered around the sanctuary, mostly friends from work and church. On the first row, Mom dabbed at her eyes with a tissue. Next to her, Thomas and Denise beamed at her with proud smiles, their hands clasped together. In the second pew, Senator Webb's arm encircled the lovely woman Nikki recognized from newspapers as his wife. She could hardly believe an important man like Adam Webb had accepted the invitation to their wedding.

Joshua, adorable in the miniature suit that matched his daddy's, watched the ceremony with solemn eyes from the vantage point of Ben's arms. Nikki smiled at her son. He was on his best behavior today. Well, aside from the near tantrum when they'd tried to pry him away from his daddy earlier.

"What token of love do you offer to one another?" The minister's question boomed in the nearly empty sanctuary.

Ben put his face close to Joshua's ear and whispered. The little boy nodded, dug a chubby hand in his pocket and pulled out a ring. Eyebrows drawn down in extreme concentration, he gave it to Ben.

Nikki extended her left hand. Her fingers trembled, not from nerves, but from the incredible joy that refused to stay confined inside her today. She searched Ben's face and saw the same joy reflected there as he spoke the words he had prepared.

"Nikki, my love for you is as deep as the ocean and as constant as the tide. As I place this symbol of my love on your finger, I join my life to yours, for now and always."

As deep as the ocean. With a perspective that most people would never have, Nikki knew the fathomless depths Ben referred to. The ring slipped onto her finger, warm and solid and precious.

She took Ben's ring from its resting place on her thumb. Ben shifted Joshua from his left arm to his right. His eyes shone with tears as he extended his hand to her. Nikki's throat was so full of love she wasn't sure she could speak the words she wanted to say.

"Ben, today we exchange rings as symbols of our love. But I gave you my heart long ago, and I've never taken it back. I never will." She blinked back her own tears and poured her love into her voice. "As I place this ring on your finger, I marry the love of my life and pledge myself to you, today and always."

When she slid Ben's into place, he opened his hand and entwined his fingers with hers.

The minister's voice, soft and vibrant, filled her ears. "Inasmuch as Ben and Nikki have consented together in marriage before this company of friends and family and have pledged their faith, they are now joined as one. And so, by the power vested in me by the State of Oregon and Almighty God, I now pronounce you husband and wife." He smiled at Ben. "You may kiss your bride."

Nikki's heart thundered as Ben drew her close. His soft lips touched hers, and she surrendered to their first kiss as husband and wife while their wedding guests applauded.

Joshua joined in, his little hands clapping with enthusiasm. When the applause died away, he asked in a piping voice that carried to the back of the sanctuary, "Can we have cake now?"

Ben and Nikki's laughter melded together.

"Yes, we can have cake now," Ben told their son.

His arm slipped around Nikki's waist, and she breathed in the fresh, clean scent of him. Their future stretched before them like an ocean, as exciting and beautiful and full of life as the crystal clear waters where they'd met. They'd dive together, side by side, into the deep.

* * * * *

Dear Reader,

Since I'm an avid scuba diver, I always said I wanted to write a book with a diving theme so I could indulge in some exciting research trips. I finally got to do it! While I was writing *Into the Deep,* my husband and I spent a relaxing week in a condo in Key West, much like Nikki's. I enjoyed re-creating some of the sights in this book such as the Cookie Lady and the clown on stilts at Mallory Square. We didn't get a glimpse of the illusive "green flash," though. If you go, be sure to ride the Conch Tour Train, visit Hemingway's home and watch for the famous six-toed cats.

We also spent a delightful time in Mexico. Cozumel has long been one of my favorite places for scuba diving because of the incredibly clear water and gorgeous underwater scenery. Though we have seen a few harmless sharks while diving, I'm thankful we've never encountered the dangerous ones that Nikki and Ben see. I have to admit, that might make me think twice about going down again.

I hope you'll let me know what you thought of my book. Please take a moment to contact me through my Web site—www.VirginiaSmith.org.

Virginia Smith

QUESTIONS FOR DISCUSSION

1. Which character in the novel did you most relate to and why?

2. Why did Nikki hide her pregnancy from Ben? Was she right to do so?

3. Ben has chosen to live a carefree life with little responsibility and no emotional entanglements. Why?

4. When Ben finds the flash drive in his apartment, he does not contact the Mexican police. Should he have done so? Why or why not?

5. Nikki goes on the dive with Ben even though she doesn't want to. Have you ever done something you didn't want to do for similar reasons?

6. When Nikki and Ben are stranded in the ocean, their prayer for help is answered immediately. Does God really answer prayers like that? Have you ever received in instantaneous answer to an urgent prayer?

7. Why did Nikki first start attending the church in Cozumel? Have you ever been driven to seek spiritual comfort when faced with a frightening situation?

8. The illegal drug and gun trafficking described in

this book are frighteningly real. Does that surprise you? Have illegal drugs impacted your life in any way?

9. Nikki was guilt stricken when she realized she endangered her son by trusting someone she had only known a short while. Ben tells her, "Women make friends quicker than men." Have you found this to be true?

10. Pastor Thomas referred to God as his "heavenly Dad." How did Ben react to that? What title do you use to refer to God?

11. By the end of the story, Ben discovers some of the consequences of the lifestyle he has chosen. Discuss those consequences and the incidents that brought him to realize them.

12. Which location visited by Nikki and Ben sounded the most interesting to you, Key West or Cozumel? Would you like to visit there one day?

13. Did you learn anything about scuba diving from this book? Would you ever give it a try?

Love Inspired.
SUSPENSE

TITLES AVAILABLE NEXT MONTH

Available November 9, 2010

LARGER-PRINT BOOKS!

**GET 2 FREE
LARGER-PRINT NOVELS
PLUS 2 FREE
MYSTERY GIFTS**

Love Inspired®
SUSPENSE
RIVETING INSPIRATIONAL ROMANCE

Larger-print novels are now available...

YES! Please send me 2 FREE LARGER-PRINT Love Inspired® Suspense novels and my 2 FREE mystery gifts (gifts are worth about $10). After receiving them, if I don't wish to receive any more books, I can return the shipping statement marked "cancel". If I don't cancel, I will receive 4 brand-new novels every month and be billed just $4.74 per book in the U.S. or $5.24 per book in Canada. That's a saving of over 20% off the cover price. It's quite a bargain! Shipping and handling is just 50¢ per book.* I understand that accepting the 2 free books and gifts places me under no obligation to buy anything. I can always return a shipment and cancel at any time. Even if I never buy another book, the two free books and gifts are mine to keep forever.

110/310 IDN E7RD

Name	(PLEASE PRINT)	
Address		Apt. #
City	State/Prov.	Zip/Postal Code

Signature (if under 18, a parent or guardian must sign)

Mail to Steeple Hill Reader Service:
IN U.S.A.: P.O. Box 1867, Buffalo, NY 14240-1867
IN CANADA: P.O. Box 609, Fort Erie, Ontario L2A 5X3

Not valid for current subscribers to Love Inspired Suspense larger-print books.

**Are you a current subscriber to Love Inspired Suspense books
and want to receive the larger-print edition?
Call 1-800-873-8635 or visit www.morefreebooks.com.**

* Terms and prices subject to change without notice. Prices do not include applicable taxes. Sales tax applicable in N.Y. Canadian residents will be charged applicable provincial taxes and GST. Offer not valid in Quebec. This offer is limited to one order per household. All orders subject to approval. Credit or debit balances in a customer's account(s) may be offset by any other outstanding balance owed by or to the customer. Please allow 4 to 6 weeks for delivery. Offer available while quantities last.

Your Privacy: Steeple Hill Books is committed to protecting your privacy. Our Privacy Policy is available online at www.SteepleHill.com or upon request from the Reader Service. From time to time we make our lists of customers available to reputable third parties who may have a product or service of interest to you. If you would prefer we not share your name and address, please check here. ☐
Help us get it right—We strive for accurate, respectful and relevant communications. To clarify or modify your communication preferences, visit us at www.ReaderService.com/consumerschoice.

LISUSLP10R